MY
BROTHER'S
JOURNEY

ROD ROBERTS

ISBN: 0615371418
ISBN-13: 9780615371412

DEDICATION

This book is dedicated to my mother, Ernestine Violet Dortch, who raised me to believe that I could do anything if I put my mind to it. She taught me about caring for other people and instilled in me a love for books. I grew up in a house full of books, and on cold winter days when I would say I had nothing to do, my mother would say, "Read a book and learn something new." Also this book is dedicated to my father, Dezie B. Roberts, who always would sit down with me in the kitchen on Saturday mornings to talk about life, having a plan, and carrying out the plan. My dad always told me I only had one job: To go to school and to be a good man. My family played a crucial part in my development. My brother Troy and my many uncles and aunts and cousins helped in the development of my story. To every family member who reads this book, I hope you see how you helped me become a better man.

The story is fictional and semi-autobiographical and written on three levels. One is personal, showing my journey from being a hardened city boy to being a soldier to being a man. Another is about my family, especially my uncle, who was like a brother to me. He decided on not taking the journey and instead took his own life at an early age, so I took the journey with him in my mind along the way. The third is professional, highlighting my chosen career to be a spy catcher. This journey has taken me all over the world with many twist and turns. I hope that one of those levels speaks to you, the reader, in some way and that you find this story of a young man coming into manhood of benefit to your life. May you feel better about the human condition after reading this story and be inspired that where there is the will to succeed and to love one another—there is a way to be a better man.

ACKNOWLEDGMENTS

Very special thanks to all the soldiers I served with throughout my career who showed me what a defender does to protect the home front. Special thanks to my uncle CW4, U.S. Army Retired Lawrence Dortch, whose many letters to me as a youngster encouraged me to consider the military. Thanks to my grandkids Jamarcus and Kiara for believing that I would finish the book by asking every time they came by the house what page was I on. I would like to thank everyone involved with the book, from the book cover design by Marion Designs, Keith Saunders, to Roland Barksdale-Hall and Sue Pauling the editors publisher, and everyone else involved.

AUTHOR'S NOTE

CHAPTER ONE

*I*t was November 7, 2008 in Baltimore, and to Gregory Steen (known as "G"), this election would be different. He promised himself that he would take a stand for his people–the Black people he saw every day on North and Pennsylvania Avenue going and coming from work with nothing to show for all the hard work they were doing every day while the nation had just had a financial tsunami and bankers were rolling in dough. Yet, his neighborhood looked like a third world ghetto. All the praying, marching, welfare programs, enterprise zones, and economic development corporations had failed his people. The politicians had failed because they had no power; the civil rights leaders had failed because they had no power. Nobody was scared of a civil rights leader whose only demand was a seat at the table. It definitely was a Black thing because the moment he drove out into the county, there were pretty new buildings, houses, and stores. That was the reality. A change had to start, and G swore that on that day, he would make it happen.

G was intelligent, articulate, and conscientious. He knew who he was and where he was in his people's history. He worked downtown as a loan officer for Harbor Bank. He watched those with the decision-making power overlook the ghettoes of Baltimore again and again. He saw loans given out to people who never consider building a factory in the inner city. For those people living a normal life, the city of Baltimore means the following location—the downtown Inner Harbor area, John Hopkins Medical Center, Fells Point, and Camden Yards; everything else was inner city.

G first became aware of the seriousness of the desperation of his people back in 1994. His high school, Dunbar, had shoot outs, stabbings, and the occasional rape. Drugs were as easy to get as a 40-ounce Red Dog beer at the corner store, and you didn't have to be 21. There were 300 homicides that year. You could buy a gun for fifty dollars with no questions asked and no paperwork needed while a cop sat parked halfway down the street. Mostly, young Black men like him were killed. Deep down inside he was worried but not scared. He was not scared of anybody. If you were scared, you didn't leave the house, or you left town. It was a Black thing to walk out the door with your head up. You were telling the world you are not afraid. G was aware there was always the possibility he might get killed over some stupid shit. So, he watched his back wherever he went and avoided the knuckleheads like the plague.

His mother Althea was a beautiful Black woman born and raised in Baltimore. She worked for Baltimore Gas and Electric Company as a customer service technician making about $35 grand a year. It was enough for the two of them, but G wished his father were still alive. In 1990, his father John had been partying at Volcanoes, a local club on Green Mount Avenue, when a hail of bullets intent on some other brother took him away. His Uncle Bobby then took on the role of raising young Gregory into manhood. Bobby had been in the Army, seen the world, returned to Baltimore, and married his high school sweetheart

Melody, Althea's sister. Bobby would talk to Gregory about courage, honor, and struggle. G had a couple of other uncles who stopped by the house, but they had not found it in them to be a mentor. Usually they wanted something from Althea—some money, a hot meal, or a place to spend the night. They were always talking about making it big but never quite got there.

G recalled October 15, 1995. The drive down to D.C. was unbelievable. He had never seen that many Black men in his life. The Baltimore Washington Parkway was packed with cars. Uncle Bobby and G brought their cameras and took pictures of everything. Unbelievably standing in the crowd of a million young and old Black men, Gregory and Bobby listened to speeches about brotherhood, doing for self, stopping drugs, and most importantly stopping the killing–stop killing your brother, your sister, your mother, and your father. G realized that life was a journey toward reaching God, and control of self is was what was required. So, from that day forward, Gregory committed to live the pledge he had taken, to not hurt or harm his brother and to respect the Black woman.

After the speeches, he went back to Baltimore and started taking his classes more seriously and, to his surprise, he became a pretty good student. His English teacher Ms. Johnson pulled him aside and asked him what caused him to change. G told her he was on a mission to make something out of his life. She told him she would help him and was proud of him. She hugged him and told him God would reward him for fighting the good fight.

Althea also noticed a change in her son. He had been depressed after the death of his father, and she was worried about him falling into the wrong crowd. She prayed for him every night and was trying her best to get promoted at her job so she could buy a house out in Baltimore County. She had heard from her coworkers that the schools were safer there, and G would not have to go through the daily survival hoops she knew he was at Dunbar High.

When she looked at Gregory, she saw John her husband. G was much like his father–tall, quick witted, brown skinned, and muscular, with a devious smile. She missed John and cried every night after he was killed. She blamed herself for not going with him to the club that night, thinking maybe just maybe she would have seen the trouble brewing over in the corner where the wanna-be gangsters were drinking too much and had smoked too much weed out in the parking lot. She thought she would never forget the knock on the door by the police that night. When she opened the door, the look on the White and Black officers' faces said it all. Gregory was there crying because she was crying, not yet knowing that he had seen his father alive for the last time just a few hours ago. Then, John was hugging Althea in the kitchen, and Gregory's image of his father was set for the rest of his life on that night—his dad hugging his mom and kissing her on the neck, the two of them laughing, while she said not to worry because dinner would be ready in a few minutes.

In June of 1997, G walked across the stage to pick up his high school diploma. He felt a degree of personal satisfaction because the many nights he had stayed up studying was about to pay off. He thought about so many of his classmates who had made excuses and quit. Some had unfortunately not made it to graduation alive. One had been killed over a jacket. Another had been murdered over a drug deal gone wrong. Both were popular young men, yet just like that they were gone forever. Although G didn't know them personally as they were not in his inner circle, he knew them. They had gone to elementary and middle school together. He had grown up with them, and they were a part of him because they were familiar faces. G knew from talks on the weekend with Uncle Bobby that it took determination to apply one's self to stay home and study for tomorrow's test. Bobby told him that in the real world some people doubted your ability to think. They watched TV, saw criminal behavior on the news, and thought all Black people were like that. Of course there were some who didn't think like that, but they would drop you like a hot potato at the first sign of trouble. Just look at the O.J. Simpson trial and what one of the family friends testified about the brother: "O.J. looked very mad and dark like he was ready to kill as he sat at the back of the kids' recital." The next person testified he was happy and smiling and produced a picture of him standing with his kids, looking like a very proud father.

Every weekend G and Uncle Bobby would get together to see either the Coppin State or Morgan State football, basketball, or volleyball teams compete. They would go to cultural attractions like the museum downtown, and on occasion they would take a ride down to the Library of Congress down in D.C. where there are more books than anyone could imagine. Bobby was a big-time reader and always had a book with him.

Bobby talked about the keys to a successful life that he believed to be universal. Laws, he said, were from the Creator himself. Seek knowledge; always try to learn something new. Respect people, as they are all unique and can teach you something. Avoid drugs, alcohol, and smoking cigarettes. G's mom had seen him smoking one day and told Bobby. Bobby made G eat a whole pack of cigarettes. After that, G had a terrible stomachache and never smoked again. Other words of wisdom from Bobby: Defend yourself with everything you have inside when threatened by a bully or a hood. Love yourself and your people so much that you won't let anyone misuse or abuse you or them. G took these talks to heart and started becoming an enlightened brother.

G had three good friends. Richard, Danny, and Napier all lived around the corner on Euclid Street. They were all determined to go to college, and they had become close over the last two years because they were all determined to graduate and go on to become something in this world. Napier wanted to be an entertainer. He sang and played the keyboard very well. Napier was on his way to New York, to the fine arts school where many of Baltimore star singers and actors had gotten their education there. Napier's parents were making enough to get him through school. Richard was good in math and his father knew somebody, so he got a scholarship to Ball State in Indiana. Danny was good at football and received a scholarship to Central State College in Ohio.

G told Napier, "I don't have enough money to pay for college, so I'm joining the Army for a couple of years. My Uncle Bobby says I can learn about what it takes to build a nation and what real men will do to protect the most important thing in life—your freedom. He also told me, 'You can't do nothing for yourself dead or in jail never forget that,' so I'm taking the opportunity to go and see the world, and then attend college."

The sad thing was they were the only four out of the guys in their clique who were serious about going on to college. So, in September 1997, they all went their separate ways. G woke up early the day the recruiter came. When he got to the Orleans Street reception station, there were already about forty recruits there. The place was well lit and the floors were buffed and highly waxed. G was impressed. His recruiter told him he would have to take one more test about an hour long. He should do his best, because it would confirm the other test he took at the recruiting office. After that he would get a physical. The recruiter said, "I hope you have on clean underwear!" and they both started laughing.

G took the test. The sergeant who was scoring the tests called out, "Steen, you scored 130 on the GT portion of the test! You can have any job you want—are you sure about being an intelligence analyst?"

G said, "Yeah, my uncle says it's a good job."

They went into another big room where there were some nurses and doctors. The nurse said, "Okay, gentleman, take off your shirts and drop your pants and underwear."

G was shocked. One of the male doctors said, "Don't be shy; everybody in the army works together. We don't hide anything from each other."

G started to laugh a little bit as he pulled down his pants. He was happy that he had on clean underwear. As the female doctor walked up to the first guy in line, G heard her say, "Turn your head and cough, and then turn around and spread 'em."

G thought to himself, "This is unreal. A female is about to hold my beans and look at my garbage disposal." He was almost ready to quit, but when she got to the guy next to him, he noticed that she was an attractive woman. She told the guy next to him turn his head and cough and then turn around and spread them. When she looked down, she said, "Somebody get a candle–this young man baked a cake!" Everybody started laughing.

When she put her hand on G's beans and he was still laughing and trying to cough at the same time, he noticed that she glanced down at his well-developed trombone, and he saw a little smile on her face. He turned around and spread his legs and did not hear any comments. He was very glad he had taken a good shower that morning.

At 5:50pm they climbed on the bus to Fort Jackson, South Carolina for basic training—eight weeks of hell. Althea had told him not to worry because he could handle anything they threw at him. Bobby was proud that G had chosen a job that dealt with computers and using your head.

The training was tough at first, but after the second week the drill sergeants seemed to back off on the harassment stuff and started concentrating on teaching them how to survive in the event they went to war. He was taught that although man throughout the course of history has attempted to live in peace with his fellow man, that he has not yet been able to do it, so the nation, the United States of America, must be prepared for war–prepared to win a war. Listening to the instructors gave him a new perspective. The Black sergeant told him that only a few hundred thousand people protected 250 million people. Hearing that their muscles, brains, and souls were dedicated to the preservation of this nation was deep. Back on the block, the gangbangers' rap was real. When you listened with your headphones on, you could hear every word. But, this was cold hard truth: Protect your freedom at all cost or lose it, and with it you lose the nation. They gave him numerous historical examples of countries that had not prepared for war and were devastated because of it, countries whose internal rivalries were used against them.

So that everybody was clear, the sergeants preached unity–no Black, no White, no Brown, no Yellow. Only being an American counted. Anything else was bullshit. They got up early every morning and went on a run of two or three miles, and when the drills were feeling good, they would run five miles. When they got back to the barracks, they had to hit the showers, and no matter what Thomas Jefferson said, all men are not created equal.

After making his bunk, it was off to breakfast for some cereal and fruit and then to classes for the rest of the day. The first day at the firing range was a trip. There was nothing quite like a firing line, with 30 soldiers in foxholes firing M-16s all at the same time. The "bang" says it all. It says, "I'm serious about defending myself, and you'd better leave me alone." Respect was given to every man that day, even the wimps, because they were armed. G walked off the firing line after qualifying, feeling like a man inside. Nobody could take his manhood away because now he respected the gun as a tool and knew that when used intelligently, it preserved freedom.

G had spotted some sisters who worked in the mess hall over the past few weeks, local girls who always seemed to put a little extra in his tray. Being 6'1" 185 pounds with handsome features was about to pay some dividends. Sandrika was the cutest one of the young ladies, and she always had something smart to say. You know the kind–Ms. Badass always talking about how "you can't handle this." Yeah, right. About the seventh week of training, the sergeants quit doing bed checks at midnight. G had her pick him up outside the barracks, and they went for a ride.

Down in the woods on the side of the road, Sandrika showed him some southern comfort he had never dreamed of. At the very moment of ecstasy, he realized he was not in Baltimore any-more. Sandrika told G that she was ready to get out of South Carolina but did not know where to go or what to do. She was 22, had no kids, and was staying with her folks. She wanted to do something exciting, not just cooking at the base twenty years from now. She did not want to join the military herself, though. That was not an option.

The local guys were plain and not doing much but working at the local textile mill. Even the ones with many years of seniority were being laid off for three and four months at a time. The men were turning to alcohol or even worse. She said crack cocaine had messed up a lot of her friends, and killings were happening all the time. G was listening to her, and for the first time, listening to a sister really opening up with what was on her mind. He told her about Baltimore and all the craziness happening there with brothers killing each other over jackets. He told her that he wanted to do something with his life and needed money for college, so he joined the army, that he would be graduating from Basic Training next week and then going on to Arizona, and that he would stay in touch and never forget that night. She smiled kissed him deeply and made him promise to never forget her, no matter what.

CHAPTER TWO

*I*t was late October. Graduation day from basic training was a beautiful day. There was a large formation of troops, and the band was playing. Families were present, and everybody was smiling. G received a certificate stating that Gregory Steen had successfully completed US Army Basic Training. G shook hands with the drill sergeants and thanked them for the time they had spent making him push himself to be better than when he showed up. Indeed, he was doing twenty more push-ups and running much faster than he did on that first physical training test they took at Fort Jackson.

From there, G was put on a bus to the airport for a plane to Atlanta. The airport was huge, much bigger than the Baltimore airport, and he could not help but notice all the sisters working in the restaurants. After a two hour layover, it was on to Tucson, Arizona. Thinking about Arizona, he imagined cowboys, Indians, and Mexicans. He had seen on the news as a kid that the Southwest was full of Mexicans who had fled the poverty of Mexico for minimum wage jobs picking potatoes, grapes, and other fruit. He put on his headphones and listened to his favorite group, 112. When the plane landed in Tucson, he noticed right away that Arizona was nothing like Atlanta.

There were four soldiers in his group headed to the Army Intelligence Center and School. One of them was going for intelligence analyst as well. His name was Kevin Kromer, a White guy from New Jersey who was pretty cool. He listened to Black music and said he went to a mixed high school and liked to shoot hoops. The other two were going to be imagery intelligence guys, and they went to a different company upon their arrival. Kevin and G ended up being roommates, which was cool for both of them since neither wanted to be listening to country music during their off time.

There was a list of rules on the bulletin board of what you could do in the barracks, and it seemed much more laid back than basic training. They were considered soldiers now and just had to be responsible, and the advanced training sergeants would leave them alone during their free time. It was a college-like atmosphere except they still had to get up and run PT every day, Monday-Friday. Every Friday the drill sergeant went through everybody's room and made sure they were clean and neat.

The classes were interesting and required doing reading at night learning all the different acronyms. The most important thing G learned from these classes was you must know your enemy, know his tendencies, and therefore be prepared to exploit them. He realized that this was really simple stuff, yet many people never do it; they just keep failing when they have a problem and never really re-looked at how they were doing things.

There were mock battles during field exercises, and he as an analyst had to brief his classmates on what had happened and what would be most likely to happen next and then provide a recommendation for a counter action. His instructors were pleased with his work and told him, "You have a future in this type of work; just keep studying. There will always be something new, and you have to know it."

Kevin and G during their free time would go over to the cactus cantina and chill out. It was the student lounge and was crowded Monday through Friday with students drinking beer, shooting pool, and trying to get to know the young ladies. G located the few sisters who came by there and introduced himself to Pam, Debbie, and Portia. They were all about the same age, 18-19, and from big cities. Pam was from Detroit, Debbie from Chicago, and Portia from Atlanta. They would all sit at the same table order up some pitchers of beer and nachos, talking about the day's events in school. It was big-time gossip about who was spending the night in so-and-so's room. G wanted to get next to one of them but could not choose because he truly liked them all. So, he decided to chill and just let whatever happen, happen.

His boy Kevin was working some honeys of his own a couple of tables over. Because Kevin was cool and hung out with G, the White girls liked him and a couple of sisters asked about him as well. G told them Kevin was cool that he was from New Jersey and that he liked Black music. He would have no problems after a strong recommendation like that from a brother. G laughed about that later that night, thinking "Kevin is in and is going to get some booty because he listens to Tupac."

G wrote home twice a week and called his mom every Sunday night to let her know he was doing okay. She said everything was going fine and there were no emergencies happening in the family right then, which meant none of his uncles were about to go to jail or had just robbed anybody. G thought about his uncles and the mistakes they had made in life. Uncle Leroy was in jail for assault with intent to do bodily harm when he had beaten a man and a woman with a crow bar over a crack argument. He was doing ten to fifteen years in prison and had left his wife and kids without a father. Uncle Thomas was eighteen when he went to Vietnam and was never the same when he returned.

Thomas has been living in shelters and working part-time jobs ever since then. He had been married briefly, but his wife could not take his always changing mood swings, so she took his son and divorced him. G never really knew what was going on inside Thomas. He had a scuffle with him once over some spaghetti. G got his point through to Thomas: "You are a guest in my mother's house, so act like it."

Uncle Sean had robbed a bank, gone to prison, robbed another bank within six months of being freed, and then was sent to prison again for ten years. Uncle Colin had been a sixties revolutionary who married a Italian girl and fathered a big beautiful family. G wondered about his cousins, so many kids, but he always enjoyed when they came to the house for the holidays. He was glad to have seen them at his going-away party. After his mental rundown of his uncles' fates, G fell asleep and dreamed of home, his mother's cooking, and shooting basketball back in the hood.

The next day he and Kevin breezed through their classes and talked with their instructors afterwards about what to expect in the real Army and, most importantly, where to get stationed. The instructors emphasized that where you were stationed was probably more important than what you were doing. Hawaii versus Kansas was a no brainer.

So, the faithful day when the assignment orders came in was a big shock to G. He was assigned to the 501st MI Battalion in Wurzburg, Germany. Immediately he asked anybody who had been to Germany what was it like and what type of duty he should expect. Everybody seemed to have a different opinion. Some loved it and said Germany was "the bomb"–good food, good sightseeing, and most importantly, "a chance to get a good BMW, at a decent price." Others said that due to the low exchange rate with the money, they could not afford much, and therefore stayed on base most of the time. Kevin was going to Korea and was cool with it. He heard both good and bad about

home, everybody was getting up and asking him where he had he been. He told them, "Down at the store walking around the neighborhood."

Althea looked at him and could see the subtle change in her son. He was becoming a man, and she wondered if he would ever truly return home. She missed him these past three and half months he had been gone. Life had gone on. Her brothers were still doing foolish things. One of her sisters had stopped speaking to her for God knows what, typical family bullshit. Only G represented something truly positive. Perhaps he would be able to pull this family together.

Althea asked, "So what's the plan for today?"

G told her he read in the paper there was a people's expo down at the Baltimore convention center, and he thought they ought to see it.

"Okay, what time are we leaving?"

"About two o'clock should be good. The doors open at twelve o'clock, and they should be rolling about then."

They got there and it was packed, literally. About five thousand people were listening to music being performed by local groups. G realized how beautiful his home girls were as they walked by with all shapes and sizes and the most outstanding hairstyles in the world. Looking at the different color hair styles, he thought purple must be hot since everybody was wearing it.

Althea was checking out the Black art on display and saw a nice picture of a Black man embracing a Black woman. Both were nude, but it was classy. "How much is it?" she asked.

The artist told her, "Normally fifty, but for you thirty is okay."

She smiled and asked, "Why thirty for me?"

He told her, "Because you're a beautiful Black woman, and one day I would like to do a painting of you, just like this one."

She could not help but blush and said, "Oh, really."

"Yes. Here is my card, and my name is Tony. Please come to my shop if you have some time and see the rest of my work."

Althea was impressed by the brother and said, "Yes, I will."

G had wandered off over by the stand selling cassettes and CDs when he saw a former schoolmate. "Hey, what's going on, McDaniel?"

"Nothing much, G, and what about you? The last time I saw you, you were joining the Army."

"Yeah, I did. I'm home on vacation for a few days, and then I'm headed to Germany."

McDaniel said, "I got a job with the Metro, helping fix engines on the buses."

"That's cool, McDaniel. You were always good in shop class; that must be your gift."

"I have to agree with you, G. I get into mechanical type stuff. College is not for me, but I will make a living and do okay. There is a school out in Columbia, Maryland that certifies mechanics. Once I get my money right, that's what I'll do."

"Sounds good, my brother. I'll see you when I get back from Germany."

G started looking for his mom and found her still over with the artist, laughing. "Are you ready to go mom?"

She said, "Yes, just a moment."

She said goodbye to Tony and promised she would stop by his shop. They walked out of the convention center onto Pratt Street and felt good about their city. There were hundreds of people walking up to go inside, mostly young, but there were some middle-aged Black people as well.

Althea asked G, "Are you nervous about leaving home again?"

He said, "Yes and no. Yes because I'm going across the ocean, and that seems like a lot of water to be flying over, and no because I'm going to see another part of the world, how other people are living. No matter what, I'm coming home, and I'm going to college and to live a good life. I want to buy you a nice house in a nice neighborhood."

Althea smiled and said, "I look forward to that day, but our house is nice as it is. It's the foolishness and waste outside that is the problem."

The days flew by so fast G could not believe the day to leave had finally arrived. He was packing his bag for the third time, trying to get his music situated. He did not want to be without some good music over there.

Bobby was waiting in the living room. "What time is your flight, G?"

"Five o'clock, but I have to be there two hours early for check-in."

Althea kissed him at the door, hugged him tightly, and whispered in his ear, "Be safe, and come home as planned."

G told her, "Yes, no problem, Mom. Eighteen months and then I'm back in the States somewhere to finish the rest of my time in the Army. Then I'm back here to go to college, all right?"

"Okay," she smiled, "that's a plan."

Bobby helped him with his bags. "Boy, what you got in this duffel bag, every piece of music you own?" he said, laughing.

"Well you know most of that is my Army gear, but I could not leave my good music to gather dust."

They took the same route back to the airport, maneuvering potholes like on a safari. Bobby gave some advice. "Be careful driving over there. The Germans drive real fast, much faster than we do. If you're not in a Porsche or big BMW, stay in the right lane. Don't drink beer over there; it will turn you into an alcoholic. There will be festivals every other month where all they do is drink and drive."

"Anything else, Uncle Bobby?"

"Yeah, expect the worst, and everything else will be a surprise."

They arrived at the airport and it was busy. G had to stand in a long line at the terminal; there was going to be a lot of people on this flight. There were a lot of fresh faces, so he gathered they must be right out of school as well. He checked his bag and went through security. He noticed the sisters working the x-ray machine, and it appeared they noticed him. He got all smiles from everybody. G thought to himself, "I hope there are some sisters over there; I need to be with some sweetness."

He bought a newspaper and a sport magazine so he could have something to read on the plane. While waiting on the plane he read in the paper about local murders and politics at city hall. Mayor Schmoke was being criticized for the failing schools, poor police work, and general incompetence of city government.

G thought to himself, "There has got to be a better way, but how?" He turned to the sports page. The Maryland basketball team had been pummeled by Duke; same old story there. Baltimore produced some outstanding basketball players, but only a few went to Maryland. All the local gurus wanted to know why Black ball players went elsewhere. G thought he knew why. It was the same thing that caused him to join the Army–to see something different, to learn something about yourself.

G went up to the counter, presented his boarding pass, and asked the young lady why he did not have a seat number. The lady explained that on military charter flights, you are given a number and they board by number; you pick your own seat.

G said, "Is that so? Thank you very much."

So, the next task was to ensure getting a window seat. With briefcase in hand, he boarded when they called sixty and higher. He found a window seat, took out his headphones and a couple of tapes, and got situated with his newspaper and *Sports Illustrated*. The 757 was huge, about three hundred seats or more. He spoke to the stewardess and asked how long the flight was.

She smiled and said, "About six hours–no time at all."

G said thanks and got comfortable in his seat. There was nobody in the middle seat yet, and he hoped it stayed that way. There was an older guy sitting in the aisle seat. When he sat down he seemed to be in his own world, so G did not try to talk to him. The water could not be seen from how high they were flying, and that was a little disappointing. He sat there thinking that his forefathers had traveled across the ocean in a terrible fashion, in the bottom of a ship, not being able to see where they were or where they were going. He put on his headphones and went to sleep.

When he woke up there was a movie showing, but he did not pay any attention to it. There was a little map in the airline magazine with Europe on it, and he pictured they must be close to England. He could not believe it himself. The movie went off, and the stewardess came by collecting cups. She told him about forty more minutes until they arrived. G thanked her and began looking out the window. I t was daybreak, and he could see cities as they passed below. There were lots of little houses everywhere. The plane touched down, and the pilot announced, "Welcome to Frankfurt, Germany!"

CHAPTER THREE

*T*he terminal was full of people in uniform. They had land-
ed at the military side of the Frankfurt airport known as Rhein
Main, AFB. There was a sergeant with a sign for new arrivals, so
G and all the fresh faces followed him. They put their bags on
little carts and went across the street to the replacement center.
The place was bustling with activity, soldiers everywhere.

G stood in line, and when he got to the front the man dressed
in civilian clothes asked for his orders. The man looked at them,
looked at his book, and said, "You're headed to the 501st MI
Battalion, Dexheim."

G stated, "I thought I was going to Wurzburg."

The man told him, "It's about twenty minutes to Wurzburg
from Dexheim."

G nodded, and the man said, "You have a couple of hours
before they come pick you up. Be back here by 11:00 am.

G walked outside and looked at the barracks. They appeared
to be fairly new, painted in brown, which gave the place a drab

look. He walked over to the PX, which had all the latest newspapers, magazines, and some up-to-date music, but not the good stuff. G was now glad he had brought his music with him.

G returned at the appointed time. The sergeant approached and called out for Steen. G spoke up, "Over here, Sergeant."

The sergeant smiled and said, "Get your bags. We have about a forty-five minute drive if traffic is good. My name is Sergeant Jones." They jumped into a little van and got onto the Autobahn. Yes, indeed, the Germans drove really fast.

G asked Sergeant Jones, "What is the 501st like?"

Sergeant Jones said, "Not bad; we're getting ready to go to Bosnia in two months, so we're training up for that. I got to tell you since you're new to the unit and other people have already been there once, some twice, you're definitely going down range to the box."

G asked him, "Why do they call it the box?"

Sergeant Jones told him, "Because once you're there, you're locked in until they let you out."

G began to think, "This is the real deal I'm already being sent to a dangerous place, and I'm new to the game."

They drove through some pretty countryside and arrived at the entrance of the small little kaserne, Dexheim. Sergeant Jones started pointing things out to G. There was a little PX, post office, mess hall, and up the road the MI Battalion compound, which was surrounded by a fence with several new looking barracks and a headquarters building. They pulled into the lot. There were soldiers walking everywhere.

Sergeant Jones said, "Let's go in and sign in with the S-1 admin office."

They went inside and talked to Sergeant First Class Matthews, a Black female who ran the shop. She was a good looking woman of about thirty-five. She looked at G and said, "Hello, Private Steen, how are you?"

G said, "I'm fine, Sergeant."

"You're going to Alpha company. First Sergeant Cummings is your top NCO. You will meet him later on today."

G nodded. She gave him some paperwork to fill out to get his pay started and get him on the 501st rolls. After filling out the paperwork, they took G over to the barracks. Luckily, he got a room to himself. Seems half the battalion was in Bosnia.

Late that afternoon G met the first sergeant, who asked him where he was from and how he had liked his training at Fort Huachuca. G told him a little bit about himself and that he had done well at Huachuca.

The first sergeant replied, "That's good because I'm sending you down range with the next group to Bosnia. I know you'll like it because it's the real world, and they're saving people's lives down there. So go through the training we're giving over the next month and be ready to go the next month."

G walked back to his room. It had a college dormitory feel to it. There was a day room with a big TV pool table, couches, books, and magazines. The gym was down the road not very far. G opened his door, laid on the bed, and took a two hour nap. When he woke up it was midnight, but he was wide awake so he started to unpack and get everything arranged the way he wanted. About two o'clock in the morning he realized he better go to sleep since he still needed to do more in processing in the morning.

His little clock rang at 6:00am. G jumped in the shower, did a quick shave, and was over at the mess hall by 7:00am. It was not a big place like a small restaurant. He signed in, and the girl behind the counter said, "Good morning. Are you new here?"

G said, "Good morning and yes, I'm new. I arrived yesterday."

"My name is Deborah. I'm in the signal company. Welcome to Dexheim."

G said, "Thanks, and I hope to see you around, too."

He made it over to the chow line, and the food was not the best looking. The scrambled eggs did not look good, so he told the cook to make his over easy. At least the fruit was fresh, so he grabbed two oranges and sat down and ate his breakfast. One nice thing about the place was the big screen TV with CNN on it. Watching the news from back home was cool.

CHAPTER FOUR

*B*ack in Baltimore, Althea was trying to get used to the fact that G was in the real world now. Her baby was in the Army, and overseas. Where had the time gone? It was just yesterday he had been born. Since John's death she had sworn off any serious relationship with another man. She had a son to raise. On occasion she had slept with an old boyfriend from high school. His name was Derrick, and they had been friends as youngsters. He had seen her at church two years after John's death. He was kind and spoke almost in a whisper whenever they met. He had a house on the West side, up in the Northwood area. He invited her over and told her she could come by any time she just needed to get away. At first, she said, "Thanks, but no thanks." But, after a couple of days of thinking about it, she came to the conclusion that she was human flesh and blood and needed to be held and loved.

The first time Althea called him and asked, "Do you mind if I stop by for a little while after work just to chill and see what a bachelor's house looks like?"

Derrick laughed and said, "Most definitely it's okay, and I am open to any suggestions or improvements you might have."

So, about six thirty, Derrick heard the knock on the door, and he rushed to open it. As he looked at her standing there, a fine beautiful Black woman, his only thought was, "This woman needs love."

Every Sunday, he would watch her in church, and her every move would captivate him. When their eyes would meet, his were saying, "Althea, I want you," and her eyes were saying, "I want you, but I don't think I should." So, he invited her in and escorted her around the house, telling her how he bought a house rather than an apartment because he wanted a home. She was impressed by his decoration of the place. He had a nice carpet and very powerful paintings including a Black woman with a skirt on, with her breast exposed and her hair wrapped in an African headdress. It was a sexually-provocative painting.

As she took a sip of the white zinfandel he had on ice, she relaxed and sat on the soft leather couch. Derrick asked her if she was tired, and she said yes. He asked her if she was comfortable with the thought of him giving her a massage. She thought about it and knew in her heart that she had come to his house to be held, to be loved, so she said yes, it was okay. Derrick told her to go to his bedroom where there was a robe hanging on the door and to put it on. He would be getting her shower started down the hall.

She walked up the flight of stairs in front of him. She could feel his eyes watching the swaying of her hips. It had been a long time since she felt this way. It turned into a wonderful night, but it would be the last. A little voice inside told her to call the artist she met at the Black Expo and see if he was for real.

CHAPTER FIVE

G had finished his processing early that day and went by the gym to see what was going on. The fellas were shooting basketball, so he decided to join them. G put on an athletic display by hitting some nice outside shots, and then he surprised them all with a dunk. They were impressed and asked him if he was a baller, and he told them no, he was actually a better football player, but he could play basketball as well. He had a good time and made some friends. He went back to his room and took a shower and told himself, "This is going to be okay."

Training began Monday morning. Alpha Company had PT at 0630 hours in the morning. They did some stretching, push-ups, and sit-ups, and then a two mile run. it was no problem, and the classes started at 0900 hours. They were about the systems being used in Bosnia and the various reports they were producing. After two weeks of classes, they went on a practical exercise for one week, and then they were certified as deployment-ready. The company commander gave a speech at the end and said how he looked forward to the challenge of twelve months in Bosnia. He was going for a twelve-month tour and was confident they could do the job and bring everybody back alive.

G keyed in on that and liked what he heard about safety first. As everyone boarded the bus, G sat with a couple of friends he had made–Private Johnson and Private Dumars. They planned to stick together for the six-month tour they would have to do in the box. It was going to be a long bus ride through Germany, Austria, Hungary, Croatia, and then Bosnia. They left about 1730 hours in the afternoon. G had a window seat. Germany was really pretty farmland everywhere with neat rows of grape vineyards everywhere. The BMWs and Mercedes were zooming down the Autobahn, and the occasional Porsche would blow by. It was sort of uncomfortable after a couple of hours just sitting there, but the bus driver said he would stop at midnight for thirty minutes.

G put on his headphones and fell asleep. Early the next morning, everybody was wide awake when the bus driver said, "We're in Hungary, a couple of hours from the base called Tazar."

The bus entered the base which was full of activity. Soldiers leaving Bosnia were there with all of their equipment, along with units headed there with all of their equipment. They had a one hour break to wash up and get some breakfast. The mess hall tent was full of GIs laughing and joking around, and G could feel the place was alive. There was a music video playing on a big screen TV showing a station from back in the States. All eyes were on the ladies dancing in the background. The Hungarian ladies behind the counter serving food were friendly and seemed to be speaking a version of pig English, using slang they had picked up from the thousands of soldiers passing through

After a while they went to a tent where some personnel specialist called out everybody's name and verified they were going to Bosnia. From that point forward they would be escorted by armed MPs in Humvees. A Humvee was sort of like an armored Chevy Explorer without all the nice stuff. They loaded up and took off upon crossing the Hungarian Croatian border where they had to put on their flak vests and helmets. Croatia was actually very pretty; it looked a lot like Germany, with neat houses and very clean streets.

As they approached the Bosnian border, however, there was a dramatic change in the scenery. At the Brcko Bridge pronounced (Birchko), there were lots of Serbian policemen, and American soldiers. The Serbian policemen were stopping all cars and asking for identification of passengers. The Americans were waved through, and G saw a war zone first hand–houses with blown off roofs, bullet holes in almost every building. Signs stating, "Land mines: Do not enter" were everywhere. The mood was solemn on the bus. All the laughing and joking stopped, and all eyes were on the people walking to work or to the shops on the street. They looked like regular people, but there was a kind of depression look in their faces. The kids waved at the bus, but the adults looked weary.

About thirty minutes later they approached the American base called Camp McGovern. Surrounded by farmer fields, it stuck out like a fort from an old western movie. They only stopped for about thirty minutes and then were on their way to Eagle Base, headquarters for all the Americans. When they finally arrived at Eagle Base, it was about 1600 hours, and everybody was tired. They went into a tent and received a welcome briefing from a personnel specialist. The personnel specialist warned them to be careful where they walked. Because they were still finding land mines on the camp, it was important to stick to the walking paths. He said that there would be someone from their unit to pick them up in about thirty minutes. G walked outside to look around. There were large tents everywhere; one of the other soldier, called it "tent city." That would be their home for the next six months.

A staff sergeant came over, introduced himself, and told everybody to grab their gear head over to tents twenty seven and twenty eight. G walked in twenty seven and threw his duffel on the wooden bed nearest the back. He had been told in Germany never to sleep by the front of a tent because when the door opens, all the cold air rushes in. He had a few minutes until the next formation, so he started to unpack. His buddy Dumars grabbed the bunk across from him, so they were happy with the living arrangements already.

At the formation everybody was just glad to be off the damn bus. It was chow time, and the sergeant was about to lead the way to the chow hall. He told everyone, "Whatever you do, do not set your weapon down. Take it with you everywhere you go. If somebody can grab it, they will, and you will receive an article 15 and get extra duty."

When they got inside, the place was lit up like Christmas. It was very bright and food was everywhere on hundreds of tables. There were already about five hundred people inside eating. All the new arrivals sat together and talked about their feelings about actually being in the box. G admitted that he was nervous on the inside but not scared.

After chow they went back to the tent, and the sergeant showed them where the bathroom and showers were at the end of their tent section He said he would be back to get them at

0830 hours to take them through in processing.

CHAPTER SIX

*B*ack in Baltimore, Bobby was working hard every day and just getting by. As he thought about G and what type of man he was developing into, he thought about his own life. He was in his early forties and wishing he could have figured out the system in America. He had done all the right things in high school–joined the Army for three years, saw the world, and returned home to marry Melody. They had a modest house, full of love, and the one child they had together (his baby girl, Marilyn), was now fourteen and starting to blossom. He guessed that he cared so much about G because he was the son he never had. Melody had not been able to have any more children due to cervical cancer. He told her it didn't matter, that God had blessed them with a beautiful daughter.

On the weekends Bobby would go to the gym, work out, and shoot basketball with guys from the neighborhood. After the games they would talk about their jobs and what the climate was like. Most had the same opinion, that if you didn't have a college degree you always had to watch your back from some new guy being brought in to manage the section. Most of them worked for the government in some form or fashion, from the post office, social work departments, and of course the police. Very few worked for any of the major companies in Baltimore. Checkout downtown Baltimore any day of the week and you will see ten sisters working for every brother. Bobby knew the system was fixed, and so did every Black man at the gym. But, they were survivors and respected one another for taking care of family.

Bobby, just like any other brother, was fighting the demons inside to just say, "Fuck it; I'm going to care only about myself." Sometimes he would think he could make it a lot easier on his own. He knew the ropes, and there were some fine sisters walking around that he wouldn't mind getting with. Then he would think about Melody and Marilyn and come to his senses. Time to go home and drink some cold lemonade, rest his aching feet, and have some dinner.

CHAPTER SEVEN

*T*o the sound of "Born in the USA" over the speakers on base, G woke up at five thirty, turned on his little flashlight, and grabbed his shaving bag and a towel. The shower water was good and hot, and he whispered, "Thank God. Having to take a cold shower would be just too much." He had been told horror stories about cold water, bathrooms not working, and heaters not working. He hoped all that would turn out to be nothing but hype.

G was ready for in processing and had all his paperwork ready, and it went very smoothly. He was brought over to the ACE and was introduced to everybody in the section. They were glad to see the new group; that meant they would be leaving after a two-week crossover. He sat down at the computer terminal that would be his, and it was just like the one at Fort Huachuca. G was a happy man and said, "I can do this" to himself.

He was shown around the entire intelligence section of the headquarters so he would be familiar with everything. In the combat camera section he saw a fine sister girl, working on some paperwork. He made eye contact and said hello. She said returned his hello and smiled, a good sign as far G was concerned. He would find a reason to return to combat camera, yes indeed.

G had some free time, so he walked around the base camp to learn exactly where everything was. He found the break room, which was several trailer homes combined. Inside was a sandwich shop, a Baskin Robbins Ice Cream Shop, and a video rental store. There was a room with a large screen TV and about fifty sofa chairs. The place was jammed with soldiers watching a movie. G asked a soldier if the place was always this crowded.

"Yes, nobody wants to be in the tents when they're off duty. So it's here or at the gym."

That night while laying in the tent, G heard the sirens going off and people running outside the tent. Apparently the Americans around Camp McGovern had been attacked by some Serbs at a television station. Several were wounded, and now the base was on full alert. G felt a tightening in his throat as a sergeant hollered at everybody in tent twenty seven to grab their gear and follow him to the bunker. Immediately, they called out everybody's name for accountability.

G heard a popping sound and asked a sergeant, "Was that gunfire?" and the sergeant said, "Be quiet." Then they heard it happening again. "Oh shit!! My second day in the country and we're fighting already," G thought.

"Lock and load your weapons!" screamed the sergeant. "We've got the perimeter on the right of the bunker. Space yourselves five feet apart. Shoot to defend yourself, but make damn sure you know what you're shooting at!"

They rushed out the bunker one by one and did as they were told, weapons locked and loaded. There were voices everywhere, people hollering out their names, shouting, "Coming through– don't shoot!"

As G lay on his stomach in the darkness, his eyes adjusted and he could see people running and hear gunfire in the background. His heart was beating one thousand times a minute, and he was sweating hard. Then a large boom sounded about 100 meters to the right. "Oh shit, that was a mortar round! These people are really trying to kill us!" G thought. G fired about ten shots in front of him. He thought he saw somebody about a hundred yards out with a gun. G did not know if he hit anybody, but he was not going out without a fight.

The sergeant came up behind G and said, "Hold your fire." After about another thirty minutes of gunfire in the distance, it became totally quiet. G could only think about his mother and Baltimore. He really wished to be sitting on his front porch right now instead of being in Bosnia during a battle. The all clear siren went off. Everybody returned to the bunker.

The sergeant said that the infantry was tracking the Serb attackers and had increased the guard force. There had been no casualties on either side. Everybody should go to bed and get some sleep because tomorrow would be a long day.

CHAPTER EIGHT

*B*ack in Baltimore, Althea read in the *Baltimore Sun* about the attack by Serbs on American forces in Bosnia. Her heart was beating as the article talked about the seriousness of the attack. It appeared to be well planned, and the intent was to force the Americans out of Bosnia. There were no fatalities, thank God. G would call as soon as he could. She was sure of that. Things were moving along fine at work, and she was thinking about taking some night classes in business management at Baltimore Community College.

It was about 9:00am in the morning. Althea went through her purse, found her little black phone book, got Tony the artist's card out, and called his shop. She asked, "May I speak to Tony?"

"Speaking," he replied.

She said, "You may not remember me, but my name is Althea. We met at the Black Expo the other day."

Tony replied, "Of course I remember you. How could I ever forget as beautiful a woman as you?"

She laughed and said, "Thank you for the compliment. But do you really remember me?"

He said, "Yes, darling, I do. What's going on?"

"Well, I've been thinking about having my picture painted. But I wanted to talk it over with you before I make the final decision."

Tony said, "That's great. Would you like to do this over lunch? What's a good time for you?"

She said, "How about 12:30 in front of the Lexington Market?"

"I'll be there," he replied and hung up.

Althea smiled while sitting at her desk, thinking about her lunch date. She admitted to herself that she liked the man from that first encounter. He was so talented as an artist and a very confident man.

Althea was five minutes late, but there he was standing in front of the market on Eutaw Street, dressed nicely with a devilish smile on his face as he watched the people going and coming.

"So nice to see you again," he said.

Althea said, "You're the one it's nice to see" and smiled.

Tony held the door open for her and asked, "What do you have a taste for?"

"Oh, I could go for some fish or a salad."

Tony said, "Fish sounds good to me as well."

After picking up their order they went upstairs and sat at a table overlooking the main courtyard area below. Tony could not help but smile when looking at Althea, and she asked, "Why are you smiling?"

Tony told her, "It's not often I get to eat lunch with a beautiful woman on a beautiful day."

Althea told him, "It's not often I get to eat lunch with a handsome man" and started laughing.

Tony asked her what type of look she was aiming for in the painting. She said, "I don't really know yet. I want it to reflect how I'm feeling and to say to the world, 'This is Althea.'"

Tony went on to discuss his life with Althea, how he was just following his heart in being an artist. He had always wanted to draw; even as a child, it came quite naturally to him. His teachers in elementary and junior high always supported him and told him he had the gift. So with a scholarship, he went to Morehouse down in Atlanta, Georgia, and learned the fine art of being an artist. He said "artist" with a flair, and Althea laughed and said, "You are a gifted man in many ways."

"Thank you, my darling, I always try to be a gentleman. But I do know how to be serious when I need to be."

She asked him, "When do you have to be serious?"

He told her, "Keeping the doors open to my shop has not been easy. Not enough people appreciate art and do not want to pay the price for a painting. Everybody, and I mean everybody, wants a discount."

She told him, "I understand, and don't ever let anything bring you down. You have got your life together doing what your heart wants to do."

He looked at her and told her, "You know what my heart wants to do right now?"

She said, "What is that?"

"I want to take you out dancing tonight and show you a wonderful time."

Althea told him, "Sounds good to me. Pick me up about eight thirty."

Tony said, "Cool. Give me the address, and I'll be there."

Althea wrote it down on a piece of paper, placed it in his hand, looked him in the eye, and said, "Eight thirty." As she walked back to work, she smiled and thought, "What am I getting myself into?"

CHAPTER NINE

Gwoke-up tired, he had been unable to really sleep after the events of the previous night. He had literally one eye open until dawn. The activity on the base was heavy all night. There were long trucks zooming around and helicopters flying overhead at high speed. G could remember just a few months ago he was walking the halls of Dunbar, laughing and joking. "Now I'm in the middle of a damn combat zone at 18."

He turned on his flashlight and called over to Dumars, "Are you woke?"

Dumars said, "Yeah, I'm up and ready to get the day started. We should get to see some good stuff today in the ACE." Dumars was from Lanett, Alabama and was 18 like G.

After they got dressed and had morning formation, they walked over to the ACE and were handed some folders and told to read the reports inside. As they read them, they were surprised by the detail about the Serb paramilitary groups. Obviously somebody was watching them with great detail, thought. G remembered his instructors teaching about knowing your enemy and predicting what he will do next. G and Dumars were told to do an analysis of the group and come up with three probable actions they might take. G could not believe what he was hearing–they wanted two 18 year olds to work on this stuff.

Dumars was smiling and saying, "We've got real jobs." So, they both buckled down and read the reports again took out a writing tablet, matching names with places. Then they made a time event chart matching dates with events such as bombings, ambushes, and demonstrations. This process would take almost two weeks to do really well.

G and Dumars really felt like they were contributing something to the effort of keeping the peace. At the end of the day they would brief the officer of the day on their findings. Now the hard part was about to begin. They were supposed to predict what the paramilitary group would do next. The Chetniks as they were called were feared by the Muslims in Bosnia because of their brutality during the war. They were known to rape women and slaughter men and boys. Now they had set their sights on removing the Americans from the Balkans. It would take a dedicated preemptive strike against them to destroy their infrastructure, and G would play a role in the intelligence cycle factor.

While sitting on his bunk, G thought about home and what everybody was doing. The base had seemed to return to normal about a week after the attack. Everyone was definitely closer and looked out for one another.

G decided to write Sandrika back in South Carolina to see how she was doing. He started his letter with the usual "How are you doing?" and then he started telling her about his experiences in Arizona, about Germany, and now Bosnia. He told her how much he wished he was home going to school. He envisioned walking the campus of Morgan State University, Howard University, or some other small Black university. He asked Sandrika if she was seeing someone and to be honest because he wanted their friendship to be one of honesty. He told her that he liked her a lot and would continue to write, and whenever possible he would come back to South Carolina to see her.

The next day at work G was told he was going on a familiarization tour of the country. As an analyst, he needed to see the places in his reports. The first stop was Tuzla, the Muslim capital of Bosnia. After being slaughtered in Srebrenica by the Serbs, all the Muslims migrated to Tuzla. A small population of Serbs was there before the war, and now there was none. The city was ancient and had become a Turkish stronghold during the Ottoman kingdom. Now because of that they were fighting again an ancient fight about who was better, who was right. There were bullet holes everywhere and more cemeteries than there should have been in any city.

As G rode along on the bus, he thought that some of the neighborhoods back in Baltimore looked just like this and in many cases worse. He thought, "Why if this is a war zone, what was I living in back home? Have I been in a war zone my whole life, and thought it was normal?"

G got off the bus in Srebinica. The officer in charge started his information briefing. Srebinica was the site of the worst massacre in the Bosnian war. The city had been a multi-ethnic city before the war, but during the war the Serbs were determined to hold an ethnic cleansing of the city. The city had been declared by the United Nations as a protected site, but the UN was weak and unable to protect the Muslims inhabitants. Eventually the city was overrun, and then the nightmare began for the Muslims. Women were raped repeatedly; men were marched off never to be seen again. Approximately seven thousand men were believed to have been murdered in cold blood.

As they walked around the compound where the Muslims had been cornered hoping the UN soldiers would not surrender, G felt a shiver run through his spine. He knew the lesson well: "Never depend on someone else to fight for you." He had witnessed this cold hard truth on the streets too often. As they drove through, the Serbs had the town, but it was not worth shit. Buildings were all the same—ghettoish–and the sewers were open, stinking to high heaven. The officer told them how the international community refused to give them any aid due to their refusal to allow the Muslims to move back home. So there you have it, a city full of hate, people sitting around with no jobs, no opportunity, no hope.

G also noted this situation, that poverty had been inflicted from powerful outside forces. Money, the oil to progress, had been deliberately denied to a particular area, so the area had been redlined, as G had heard the term as a youngster concerning his neighborhood. G put this information in the back of his mind as he rode back to Eagle Base. Bosnia was such a beautiful country, with small mountains and valleys everywhere. The thought of why would they tear up such a beautiful place kept running through his mind. He would have to keep reading the history of the country and find the root to this destructive weed, G thought. "There are causes for everything. Shit doesn't just happen."

As they entered through the gate, everybody had to get off the bus go to the clearing barrel and clear their weapons. G was hungry and went straight to the mess hall for dinner. As usual, vegetable lasagna was on the menu, but there were pork chops smothered in onions with mashed potatoes and gravy as well. G spotted a couple of sisters sitting together and sat at the table behind them. Just seeing some sisters did his heart good. They looked back at him a couple of times, and then one of them said, "Excuse me. What is your name?"

"Gregory Steen, but all my friends call me G."

She said, "My name is Lakeesha, this is Faye, and this is Marsha."

G, trying to sound southern, said, "Nice to meet you. Where do y'all work?"

Lakeesha said that they were reservists from Florida in a postal unit.

G said, "Is that so? Where in Florida?"

Marsha spoke up and said, "Tampa, home of the University of South Florida."

G smiled and dropped the southern accent, asking, "Are you all in school there?"

Faye said, "Yes, we are sophomores, and now we're here. But it's cool; the GI Bill is paying our tuition."

G asked, "Do you mind if I sit with you?"

They said no problem and pulled up a chair for him. They talked about everything, from living conditions on the base to stuff going on at home. They asked him which tent he was in, and G told them tent 27; they were in 149.

G commented, "I will definitely start stopping by the post office…"

Lakeesha looked him straight in the face and told him, "That's probably a good idea."

G just smiled and said, "Good night, ladies."

The next few days went by uneventfully. Dumars and G were going to the gym after work to run on the treadmill and then lift some weights. The place was always packed with soldiers trying to relieve some stress. It was also a good place to see the fit women on base. Those gray army shorts with the black leotards up under could be quite revealing sometimes.

Dumar's was about 5'11 and 175 pounds, and he was determined he to put on ten pounds of muscle while in Bosnia. Dumars was getting to like the Army and wanted to see some stateside duty so he could buy his own car and do some cruising. College was in the picture but not necessarily the priority. If he could find a nice job without attending college, he would take it.

G asked Dumars, "How much does it take to live nice in Alabama?"

Dumars replied, "Thirty five thousand dollars, and you're living okay. G, you got to see Alabama for yourself. Little small towns, man–you don't have to make fifty thousand to live like you do up North. You can buy a nice house where I'm from for eighty thousand dollars, on a half acre lot."

G thought about that land. Now, he only knew of houses stuck together where you could hear your neighbor doing it to his girl, up close and personal.

G said, "My neighbor's name was Jalen, and I thought his name was Baby from as many times as his girlfriend said, 'Ooh!! Baby!'" G smiled, "If you know what I mean. Where has Johnson been hiding? I have not seen him for a couple of days."

Dumars replied, "Johnson has a honey already and stays by her side all the time, a good looking honey from Texas."

G said, "That reminds me, I met some honeys the other night. They're living in tent 149. Let's go over there."

Dumars said, "What do they look like? I don't want to get stuck with no fat one" and started laughing.

G smiled and said, "They're straight, my brother, kind of sassy college girls."

Dumars said, "After I shower, I'll be ready to go."

So, as they approached tent 149, they could hear the music, a little Mary J. Blige singing her heart out. G knocked on the door and a voice asked, "Who is it?"

"It's G. Is Lakeesha here?"

"Yeah, come in."

As G and Dumars stepped into the tent, they were surprised at the mink blankets on each bed. The place looked like a home, with little lamps and a little table in the middle. Lakeesha came toward them smiling, "Hello, G. You sure took your time to come see us."

G said, "I've been a little busy at work, but that's taken care of now, so I'm on the case." He smiled. This is my partner, Dumars."

"Hello, Dumars, where are you from?"

"I'm from Alabama, and I understand y'all are from Florida."

"Yes, that's true. What else did G tell you?" she inquired as she looked dead at G.

"Oh, nothing much, that you had two friends, that's all."

Marsha walked into the tent at that moment and made eye contact with Dumars. "Hello," said Dumars, and a moment later Faye walked in. Dumars said "hello" again. The girls went to the back of the tent and talked for a moment. Dumars whispered to G, "They're all nice."

G said, "I told you they were straight" and started laughing.

Lakeesha walked up and said, "What's so funny?"

G said, "Oh, nothing… what is the plan for the rest of the night?"

Lakeesha said, "We would not mind playing some cards or dominos, whichever you like the most."

G said, "I could go for some spades."

They paired up, Lakeesha and Marsha versus G and Dumars. They played cards until about ten o'clock that night, laughing and joking around talking about home. They had a good time and in the back of everybody's mind was the thought, "If we have to be here, we might as well make the best of it."

As they were getting ready to go, G told Lakeesha, "I really had a good time."

She responded, "So did I. Now you know where to find me."

G said, "Okay, I will definitely be by. What's your number at work?" She gave it to him.

Dumars told Marsha goodbye and that he would stay in touch, she told him that would be fine and gave him that look, the look that says "yes, you're my type, and we can hook up."

As the guys walked back to their tent, they gave each other a high five and said, "Yes! This isn't all bad after all."

G called Lakeesha the next day at work and asked how things were going. She said fine, and he asked her what her plans were for after work.

She said, "Nothing yet. What's up? What do you have in mind?"

G told her he wanted to watch a movie. Lakeesha told him to go ahead and rent it, and they could watch it at her place. She did not like the little movie theater on post; there were too many people and too much talking while the movie was on.

G said, Cool. I'll be there about 7:00pm."

The rest of the day at work was a blur; all G could think about was Lakeesha. When he got off from work, he walked over to the video rental store and rented *Deep Cover*, starring Laurence Fishburne. He then went back to his tent, took a shower, and put on a sweatsuit. He ambled over to her tent. As he knocked on her door, he noticed, the quietness at that moment. There wasn't a lot of movement going on in tent city.

Lakeesha said, "Come in." She was fixing the TV so that they both would be able to see it comfortably since most of the time the TV was facing her bed.

She asked G about his day, and he told her, "It was okay; nothing really stressful occurred. I'm getting the hang of it, being an analyst. And how did yours go?"

She laughed and said, "Every day at the post office is a trip. Always somebody's mail goes half way around the world before it finally gets here, and people call and complain about why it takes five days to get a letter sometimes, and four weeks the next."

G asked her about Florida and what it was like growing up there. Lakeesha told him about Tampa, how it was a small city compared to Baltimore, sitting on Tampa Bay. The Black community there was small and basically on one side of town, near downtown. There were several famous black baseball players from Tampa. Lakesha said she had a normal childhood with two brothers and one sister; her father worked at the airport, and her mother worked at the post office. She told him going to college had always been her dream, and she was going into marketing.

G listened to her intently and asked her the all-important question about a boyfriend back home. Lakeesha smiled at him and said, "Yes, I used to have a boyfriend back home. But when I went off to college, we broke up. Now I am single.

G asked her, "Was college what you thought it would be?"

She answered yes and no. The school was very big, with lots of new buildings being built everywhere, and that was nice. However, the classroom instruction was somewhat lacking; there was too much joking around in class as far as she was concerned. She wanted to learn the trade and then be a marketer for a Black company. She told G she hoped to see Baltimore for herself one day.

G smiled at her and told her that would not be a problem. He told her, "I want to go to college as well, get a degree and make some good money."

As time went on, they talked every day and grew close. The living arrangements on the base just were not conducive to romance, so they promised to meet once they both rotated back to the world. When the day came to leave, G kissed Lakeesha on the lips. He could tell that she wanted a real kiss, but he held off. He shook hands with his buddies and said his goodbyes; it was back to Germany for the remainder of his tour.

The time in Germany went by in a blur. G was promoted to sergeant, and when he received his orders for the states, he was pleasantly surprised to have gotten his home state as he had requested. Fort Meade, Maryland was printed on his orders, and he could not believe it. Fort Meade was about 25 miles south of Baltimore on a large piece of land with lots of intelligence units. G would fit right in until his time was up, and then he would go to college. He called his mother told her the good news, and she was very happy that her boy would be so close.

CHAPTER TEN

*A*lthea had been working on her house while G was away, buying nice new furniture with a modern look and feel to it. Tony had been helping with the art and other ideas. They were spending time together almost every weekend, and Althea actually felt alive again. Tony was such a breath of fresh air, a cool self-assured brother whom she could actually talk to about anything. They were sharing each other's lives with no pressure or demands, and she was happy with that. Tony liked Althea as a person and was digging just helping her find herself artistically. He had never dealt with a woman who had lost a husband and found something very spiritual about her. When he took her out dancing or to dinner, he saw her soul light up in her eyes. It was something unreal for him, so he knew he must treat her right. Althea's classes were going along fine, and all was right. Her son would soon be back home.

Bobby was still working hard and doing the same routine. He would go out every now and then, checking out the Ravens and the local college teams. He could not wait to see G. The fact G would just be down the road would be all right, as they could go to the games together just like old times.

CHAPTER ELEVEN

G made it to Fort Meade and signed into the 705th MI Brigade. He was told he would be working in the building at NSSA, also known as the National State Security Agency. Then he met the first sergeant who told him a totally different story. The first sergeant said a new program was being started and that he would actually be working in the city of Baltimore on a hush-hush project. G was excited about the prospects. He was given the address in the city where he would be working and was told to find an apartment in the city or the suburbs. He was told he would not be staying on base and that he should not even come to the base for a while.

When G arrived at the address on 3130 Eutaw Street in South Baltimore, he didn't think very much of the building. It was a six story brick building that looked about fifty years old. He met the first sergeant, 1SG, Adrian Aiken, and then he met the commander, Lieutenant Colonel James Briley, a tall well-built Black man. LTC Briley dressed in civilian clothes welcomed G to the detachment. He explained to G that the unit would be referred to as the detachment at all times–nothing more, ever. The detachment's job was to detect, identify, and neutralize foreign enemies here in the United States before they killed any Americans. G would be one of the analysts and had been hand-picked because he was from the city of Baltimore.

LTC Briley looked G in the face and told him, "No one is to know what you're really doing. Your cover story is you are helping out the recruiting office located on the first floor of the building until it is time for you to get out of the service."

G was introduced to Sergeant Kevin Randle, the senior analyst who would show G everything he needed to know. They would start first thing the next day with a threat briefing and follow that up with a current operations briefing.

G went home to his mother's house that night. When Althea asked G about his day, he was somewhat startled because he had to lie to her and tell her it was just okay, and that he'd be helping the recruiters bring in new people. "They want to use me because of my hometown background," he added.

She smiled and said, "That's good, isn't it? It's wonderful how things work out. You couldn't have planned it any better if you had tried."

He looked at her and just smiled inside and said, "You're right, Mom, the Lord is definitely looking out for me."

She asked, "Why don't you just stay here?"

G told her he needed to get his own place and get used to paying bills and taking responsibility; besides, he would only stay a few months and then move out. She agreed half-heartedly and said, "You're right; you need a place of your own so you and your girlfriend can have some privacy. By the way, what's her name again?"

G smiled at his mother's attempt to glean information from him and responded, "I don't have one–yet" with a devilish smile.

The next morning he got up early and reported to work. He caught two buses, G said to himself "I need to buy a car right away." He would look for one on this first weekend.

When he arrived at the building there were a few people standing around the entrance to the recruiting office smoking cigarettes, "G" just shook his head, smoking and the military don't work. Sergeant Randle led him up on the fifth floor to the analytical section. There were several large screens and about fifteen different computers connected to various agencies' databases as explained by Randle. The threat briefing began. G was told that NSSA had information which indicated there were probably three or four attack cells located in the Baltimore City area.

These teams on occasion made coded telephonic and computer email contact with known terrorist numbers and computers located in England, Lebanon, and Pakistan, and the detachment's job was to locate and identify the members of the attack cells before they carried out any attacks. There was a sense of urgency in the detachment. G was briefed that the detachment had 35 agents and 75 support staff. The 35 agents never came to the building for any reason. They lived and worked in the city of Baltimore, and everything they did was to try and infiltrate the foreign community of Baltimore to develop informants who would tell them who the militants and extremist terrorists were.

"These guys are good at what they do," Randle said. "They use computers to write their reports and cell phones just like the bad guys do." He had never met even one of them but had great respect for their bravery and selflessness. G's job would be to help connect the dots–phone calls, telephone numbers, meeting places, and persons of interest. His knowledge of the city would help immensely. If he thought something was unusual, he was to put it in his report. G took it all in and said to himself, "What have they gotten me into? I'm just supposed to be burning time until I get out, and now they have me doing some really important work." G said he would give it his all because he certainly did not want anything bad to happen to any of his people right here at home.

First, G needed a car, so he asked Uncle Bobby to take him around to a couple of car dealers to find him something decent but not too expensive. On Saturday morning Uncle Bobby arrived right about 10:00am. He said he knew of a couple of dealerships on Route 40 in Catonsville that should have cars in G's budget. As they were riding, G asked Bobby how things were going.

Bobby responded, "Okay. I just wish I had done what I was supposed to do as a younger man. A better education would have made a difference, no doubt."

G said, "I am thinking about taking some classes myself if I have the time. But my job helping the recruiters might keep me too busy."

G saw a nice used Altima for eight thousand dollars and said, "I can afford that. Bobby, what do you think?" Bobby agreed the price was right; the payment was going to be one hundred and eighty-eight dollars. G felt like that was a good price, so he drove it home following Bobby.

When his mom saw the car she said, "Wow, that is a nice car."

G smiled and said, "Yeah, I can take you to church on Sunday. Just need to wax it up, get some rims." They went inside to have dinner. Mom had cooked leg of lamb, and it smelled good. G just thought, "Things are working out fine. Stick to the plan, 2000 and I'm out."

Monday morning G drove to work and parked in the parking garage next to the building. He walked up the stairs to his office and saw the boards with charts and names on them. He could not believe that he was helping protect the United States of America in this way.

Randle said, "Good morning Steen, ready to get down to business?"

G replied, "Yes, Sergeant, let's do this."

They began connecting the dots. It appeared that a lot of calls were being made from the Lexington Market area using those disposable cell phones, where you use a card and buy time for it. So they drew a big circle around Lexington Market. G remembered going to the market with his mother sometimes when he was young. It was big with a lot of booths where people sold all types of food but mostly soul food, fried chicken, fried fish, and fresh meats straight from the slaughterhouse. He would ask his mom if she wanted to go this weekend so he could see it for himself again with fresh eyes.

It also appeared that a lot of calls were coming from nearby John Hopkins University, and Randle said, "They have a lot of foreign students, and no doubt some of them are connected to the enemy."

G thought to himself, "I thought John Hopkins is where all the smart people went to school–doctors and lawyers. And it turns out they have a bunch of nut cases going to school there."

At the end of the day Randle told G, "Good job, we will catch these guys."

G walked to his car and was thinking, "What a day!" But he felt good because he knew what he was doing did help the team. He drove home to his mom's house, and she was not there yet, so he turned on the TV to watch a little basketball. The Washington Wizards were playing the Atlanta Hawks. It did not look good for the Wizards. Lakeesha crossed his mind, and he thought, "Perhaps, I should give her a call."

He went through his bags and found his phone book. He dialed up her number. Her mother answered and said she was not home yet, so he left a message and the number and went back to watching the game. When his mom walked through the door, she looked tired.

G asked her, "How was your day?"

Althea replied, "Okay, typical stuff. But I'm good now. Do you want something to eat?"

G said, "No, I'm okay. I had a big lunch, and I've got to watch my weight. Can't get too fat and not be able to fit in my uniform."

Althea just smiled and laughed. "You're right. Ten more pounds and you'll be busting out of those tight pants they got you wearing." She went upstairs and G went back to watching the game.

At halftime he picked up the phone dialed Lakeesha's number, and she answered it this time. "Hello?"

G said, "Well, hello, Ms. Florida, how are you doing?"

Lakeesha burst out laughing and said, "I'm fine. And how about you, Mr. Baltimore?"

G told her, "I'm doing okay, working at a recruiting station in Baltimore until my time is up. What about you?"

"I am back in school and doing all right, studying hard and staying out of any drama."

G said, "That is the best way to go–no drama rule."

She asked, "And what about you? Has anyone tried to pull you into any drama yet?"

G knew what she was asking and replied, "Nope, ain't going to happen. They didn't have time for me before since I had no job and no car. Now that I have a job and a car, I have no time for them."

Lakeesha laughed and said, "That sounds like you know what you're doing."

G said, "You know, I was thinking after I get settled in on the job about flying down to Tampa to see you on a weekend."

Lakeesha smiled to herself. "Are you serious? You really want to see me?"

G said, "Yes I do. I will check on the price of a ticket. Give me three weeks, and I'll be there on a Friday." They talked for hours, and it was good. G just felt a connection with Lakeesha that he did not have with any of his home girls. That time together in Bosnia, the stress, and tough living conditions were something that they shared and had endured so that he really respected her. He promised to call again in a few days after checking out the flight info.

Lakeesha said, "Don't worry, I'll be here. I don't go out during the week, only on the weekends with my girlfriends."

The next day at work when G walked in, the place was busy. There had been a flurry of phone calls during the night from England and Germany to Baltimore cell phones, and it appeared people were talking in code, talking about purchasing 13 shirts and the different type of shirts, three button versus four button, green shirts and red shirts. Figuring it all out would be difficult without a key to the code. Randle asked G what he thought about the calls.

G said, "I think they're planning to hit something, and it sounds like more than just one place. Not like the Oklahoma City attack, where there was just one target."

Randle said, "I agree with that. We will put that into our briefing for the commander."

G asked, "What are our guys reporting? Is there anything from the field?"

Randle said, "The reports are these guys are doing a lot of traveling back and forth to New Jersey and New York City. They're buying counterfeit clothes and shoes selling them in the neighborhood stores and making big profits."

G had never been to New York City, but he had heard and seen the counterfeit stuff growing up in the city and told Randle, "Yes, that has been going on for a long time. Fake FUBU and other Black-styled clothes are sold down on Baltimore Street."

Randle said, "Let's take a ride; maybe we might see something in those stores out of the ordinary."

They got in his car and went down to the shopping area on Baltimore Street, and it was just as G remembered it. There were beautiful Black Baltimore women with the crazy hair styles and every color of hair imaginable. They were fine.

Randle said, "Damn, I didn't know this was where the women were" as several of them started smiling at him with their gold teeth brightly shining.

G said, "Let's check out the stores."

One by one they went inside. They went into Tim's Spot and were approached by salesmen right away since they were in uniform. G told them, "We're looking for some casual clothes for when we go to the club. Something fly, but not too fly."

The salesman said, "I understand. No bright oranges or yellows for you brothers. How about some Baltimore Blue? Yeah, that's what you two need." With that he darted into the back room and returned with some light blue pants, sweaters, and shirts.

G was impressed and said, "I like that." Randle agreed, so they bought the complete set for forty five dollars a piece. G asked, "Whose stuff is it, FUBU?"

The brother said, "Nope this is brand new. A brother named Redman from up in New York City." G said, "That's all right. I'm going to have to go to New York and pick up some of his stuff."

The salesman said, "No need for that. We got the connect already down here, a wholesaler named Achmed down on Pratt Street."

G said, "That's cool then; it will save us a trip." He looked at Randle and said, "Let's roll."

In the car Randle said, "That's going to be your new nickname."

G said, "What?"

Randle replied, "From now on you'll be known as 'Baltimore Blue.'" They both started laughing.

G said, "I like that. I think I'll use it at the clubs. We learned a lot on just that short little trip, I hope the field agents know what they're doing. I think we should tell the commander what we learned right away."

Randle said, "I agree, I knew you were going to be an asset when they told me you were from Baltimore."

When they got back to the office, they asked the commander's secretary was the commander in, and she said he was out but should be back in a couple of hours. They went back to the analysis area and started looking at the board and the map of the city. G said Pratt street really has two parts. Downtown near the financial district it has lots of banks and stockbroker offices, but outside of that there are small stores selling everything from clothes to hardware.

Randle said, "The fact that this Achmed goes back and forth to New York would be ideal cover. How much do you want to bet that he has a big van?"

G just smiled and said, "I bet he's got a box truck."

Finally LTC Briley returned, and G and Randle were ready to give their report. The colonel asked, "What do you guys have that you've been dying to tell me?"

They told him about their analysis, how they had went downtown on Baltimore Street, and they had discovered a guy with a store on Pratt street and a suspicious New York connection with some Arabs. He said, "It sounds like a lead, and the field is working another area of town." He looked them both in the eye and told them, "Sometimes just being a young soldier can get you information that a late twenties mid thirties guy just can't get. So this is the deal: Check out the store on Pratt Street without asking too many questions. Get the tag number of the truck or van if it's parked nearby. Get a business card from the store so we will have the phone number. Go back and work that salesman who sold you the Baltimore Blue outfits. Have him recommend a club and offer to let him hang out and show you two around. Can you do that without screwing it up?"

"Yes, sir!" they both replied.

The colonel gave them that look that said, "I'm trusting you don't screw this up."

G and Randle went back to their area and just could not believe that the boss had put them on the case. That's when G realized that the guys in the field were finding it tough to infiltrate these tightly knit cells. "The boss said late twenties to mid-thirties guys are too old to hang out with the folks involved. "Let's plan this out first thing tomorrow of what and how we do this."

Randle said, "Okay, I will think about it tonight and come in with some ideas. Let's meet at 9:00am."

G went home that night with a feeling of excitement just tingling in his gut. He was working on some important stuff and could not let anybody know about it, even his uncle Bobby. His mom was not home yet when he got there, so he went to his room, turned on the television, and took off his uniform. He jumped in the shower and took a long hot shower. He heard his mom shut the door when she came in. His mom called out to him, and G shouted, "I'm in the shower, Mom."

Althea said, "You can come and eat when you're through. I stopped at KFC and got us some chicken."

Althea, was tired and didn't feel like cooking. It had been another boring day on the job, and she was ready for a vacation. She had picked up a couple of travel brochures in the cafeteria at work. She heard a couple of her girlfriends talking about taking a cruise to the islands, so she told them to count her in if it wasn't too expensive.

G came downstairs saw the food on the table and the brochures and asked, "Are you going on a trip, Mom?"

Althea looked at him and realized that G had seen more of the world than she ever had, so she said, "Yes, by the way, I am. Me and my girlfriends are going on a cruise so we can see something other than Baltimore for a change."

G just smiled and said, "I understand, Mom. You deserve a nice vacation–some sunshine, sandy beaches. Just let me know if I can help."

Althea thought to herself, "First thing tomorrow, I am going to book me a cruise."

When she got to work the next day, she spoke with her friends and asked if they serious about the trip. All three of them said, "Yes, let's do it." They promised not to back out at the last minute. Then they put Althea in charge, so she called the travel agency on the back of the brochure, Century Travel in Catonsville. A nice lady answered the phone with a Jamaican accent and asked, "Can I help you?"

Althea explained what she and her friends wanted to do, to get away without spending an arm and a leg.

The lady recommended, "You can just go to Jamaica for a five day trip–leave on Wednesday and come back on Sunday, plane and hotel including breakfast for $800, $400 for air and $400 for the hotel."

Althea thought that was not bad at all, so she told the other ladies, Jean, Pam and Lisa, and asked them what they thought. They all agreed that was not a bad price. Pam said she did not know how to swim, so the idea of a cruise was not really her cup of tea.

Althea told them, "We should go within the next thirty days before the prices change." They all agreed, "Yes, let's go in two weeks before something comes up."

Althea was really excited. She put in for leave and called the lady up at Century Travel and said, "We are going in two weeks. Let's book the vacation" and put it on her one and only credit card. When Althea got home, she could not wait to tell G that she was going to Montego Bay, Jamaica. She started planning what she would wear while down there. Since the lady said it's very warm, shorts and tank tops would work along with sundresses.

She told Tony about her upcoming trip. He was pleased and told her she deserved to get away and to take a camera and lots of pictures so she could look at them for the memories of being in paradise.

CHAPTER TWELVE

G and Randle had arrived early at work but instead of being in uniform, they had on casual clothes, khaki pants and Timberland-like shoes. They both looked like some young dudes you would see anywhere in the city. They sat at the table and talked about what they would say about what they were looking for, some fly clothes without having to pay full price. If asked about what they did, they would say they were in the Army and worked at the recruiting station, keeping it simple and changing the conversation back to about clothes and clubs and women. They both agreed that would be how they played it, young bucks looking for the honeys.

They decided to drive G's Altima and they proceeded over to Pratt Street. This was not the financial side of Pratt Street; this was in the hood on the other side of the Inner Harbor across Martin Luther King Street, where the stores sold reconditioned refrigerators and stoves and there were hardware stores, pawn shops, and chicken and trout joints. There were hair braiding stands and barbershops and clothing and shoe stores and also liquor stores, one on every corner. They spotted a clothing store that had the bright clothes in the window.

Randle said, "How much you want to bet that's it?"

G said, "No bet; that's it."

They parked and walked inside. The music was bumping as they entered. A little Jay-Z was on the speakers, and a young Black salesman asked them, "Can I help you?"

They said that they had been over on Baltimore Street the other day looking for fly outfits to do some clubbing, and the guy had recommended this place, that a guy named Achmed had a direct connect with FUBU or Redman up in New York.

The salesman smiled and said, "That's right, we do have the new Red Man clothing line straight from New York. Achmed is not here right now, but I can help you with whatever look you're looking for."

G said, "That's cool. We heard about this club called Melba's on Green Mount and 32nd Street. We want to be fly when we walk up in there."

The salesman said, "I know the place well. Friday nights there are fine, plenty of sisters up in there. About 10:30pm they start rolling in, and you do need to have a certain swagger about yourself to get some attention. Let me go in the back and bring out some of the Redman stuff."

While he was gone, G and Randle looked at the place with an eye for detail. There was nothing fancy about it. There were lots of tee shirts on the racks jeans and slacks, a Black female by the register, and what looked like a camera in the corner looking over the entire shopping floor.

G thought, "The camera seems out of place, but then again maybe there is a lot of shoplifting going on in the hood."

When the salesman returned, he did have some nice stuff. There were slacks with matching shirts and belts, nice material.

Randle asked, "How much for the set?"

The guy said, "$85.00 each."

Another salesman from across the store said, "Give it to them for $75.00."

Randle asked G, "What do you think?"

G wanted to get to know the salesman better, so he said, "Yeah, 75 seems fair" and then he asked the brother, "What other clubs should we check out for the honeys?"

The brother said, "Club Choices for the young ones, and the Five Mile house for the mid twenties ones."

G asked with a big smile, "Do you have a card? We might be back if these clothes help in me getting to home base."

The brother said, "My name is David," and they shook hands.

G introduced himself and said, "This is my Army buddy Randle," and Randle shook his hand.

David, "The Army. You guys do have that clean cut look. That should help you with the Baltimore honeys as well."

G told him, "We'll give you a call. Probably be back by in a couple of weeks to do some more shopping."

David said, "Cool."

G paid the female at the register and winked at her and she smiled. He told her he would be back and hoped she would be working that day.

She said, "Monday through Friday, I'm here."

G smiled and said, "And what's your name?"

She said, "Lisa."

"So, Lisa, I will see you next time," and walked out.

The name of the shop was Martin's Clothes Store at 1902 Pratt Street, Unbeknown to them, Achmed was in town. But his store staff did not know that Achmed had another side to him. He did not tell them his every move. He had another side that he had never shown out in the public. Achmed Jackson, African American, Muslim, born and raised in Baltimore, City High School graduate, homeboy was not happy about this world we are living in.

He had grown up with his very devout father and saw everything through a prism of what was wrong with this world. He was well traveled; his father had taken him on trips to the Caribbean, Africa, Europe, and the Middle East. He had actually been to Israel and seen Jerusalem. Once they had traveled to Nigeria, and when he saw kids showering from a broken pipe outside of a building, he thought, "This world is lost with so much murdering, robbing and stealing going on." When Achmed got off the plane back in the states, he was determined to try to change this world, even if it meant killing the people responsible for this madness .

His father had left him with a million-dollar life insurance policy and the store when he passed away from a heart attack in 1998. He had not gotten the chance to say goodbye because his father died in the hospital before he could get there. Among his father's friends were Lebanese business men in New York City who provided him with clothing lines at a discount rate and fed him on a religious diet that he needed to do something for the Brotherhood. Just a few years previously, he had attended the Million Man March with his father, and he had never seen so many Black men before in unity, preaching about making this country and the world a better place.

His father had told him that day was when Islam had put America on notice—it must follow God, or be brought down. So, Achmed was planning something big with his New York friends. All the details were not finalized. He had been told to be patient but to be ready for when the time arrived.

CHAPTER THIRTEEN

*T*wo weeks later, Althea was rushing to get to the airport with Lisa because they were late leaving the house. They should have been there already. It was 6:30 in the morning, and the flight was scheduled to leave at 8:00am. When they got to BWI Airport and parked in the long term parking, they were frantic. They got inside and saw the long line of people with four and five suitcases. They breathed easier as a lady in front of them said, "Don't worry; they won't leave without us. They tell you to get here early, but the plane won't leave until 8:30am."

Then Jean and Pam showed up and said, "Wow! Why is the line so long?"

The lady told them that since people were bringing gifts with them for their families, extra luggage cost a little bit more and made ticketing take longer.

Althea thought to herself, "I can't believe I am actually going on vacation outside the country!" Hearing G talk about

Germany and Bosnia made her feel adventurous, and she was really looking forward to having some fun.

They eventually boarded, and she felt butterflies as the plane lifted off. The airline stewardesses were all beautiful young Jamaican women with nice accents. All of the ladies were all in the same row, and everybody was laughing and joking, talking about hitting the beach as soon as they get there.

After about two hours the pilot said, "We are approaching Montego Bay and will be on the ground in fifteen minutes." Althea took a deep breath and looked out the window and saw the bluest water she had ever seen, palm trees, and cars on the road looking like tiny boxes moving along. They got off the plane and picked up their luggage.

The customs man asked, "Where are you staying?"

Lisa spoke up and said, "The Doctor's Cave Hotel."

The customs guy smiled and said, "Good choice, right across the street from the beach for you lovely ladies." He added with a slight glint in his eye, "I go there all the time."

"You don't say," said Pam with a big smile, and they all laughed as they walked toward the bus stop. Althea knew already they were going to have some fun.

It was a nice 85 degrees with a gentle breeze. A man approached and said, "Air Jamaica vacations?" When they said yes, he asked for their vouchers and told them to take bus number 4. It was a short bus ride from the airport, about ten minutes, and the staff was quick in getting their luggage off the bus.

A beautiful young light skinned, long haired Jamaican girl was at the desk, maybe 21 years old, said, "Welcome to Jamaica and the Doctor's Cave Hotel."

There was a bar and swimming pool nearby, and Jamaican music was being played in the background. Althea was happy already and thought, "The travel agent was right; this is going to better than a cruise."

After checking in, they were escorted to their rooms, which overlooked the swimming pool and the main drag right in front of the hotel. There were cars and buses moving swiftly along the road, and hundreds of people walking the street. Many women were wearing their swimsuits with wraps around their waists. Lisa was Althea's roommate, and Lisa was ready to hit the beach. Their room was connected to Pam and Jean's, so they opened the door and were like one big family. Jean said she could not believe she was in Jamaica and was just smiling and shaking her head in delight.

Pam said, "You can feel the heat and the love in this place! I'm ready to hit the beach, too." They all changed into their swimsuits, wrapped on their towels, and headed across the street to the beach. The girl at the desk told them take about ten dollars with them to buy an umbrella to lay under when they were not in the water, so they did.

At the beach entrance the attendant asked where they were staying. They told him, and he said, "Welcome to Jamaica, ladies; enjoy yourselves!"

Althea could not believe her eyes. In all of her life she had never seen water so blue and clear! There were people everywhere–kids, teenagers, young adults, and even old couples, all in the water laughing and playing. She waded into the water, and it was not cold. It felt warm to the skin, and she swam a few feet into it and felt the sand beneath her feet.

Lisa was beside her and said, "Althea I'm so glad you came up with this idea. This place is beautiful."

After about forty five minutes in the water, they walked back onto the beach. Several young Jamaican teenagers approached with shorts and Doctor's Cave polo shirts and asked if they would like umbrellas to block the sun. They said yes, and they were brought and placed right away.

Pam spotted what she thought was the finest Black man she had ever seen. The tall dark slim dreadlocked man was giving people rides on a jet ski. He was riding it like a motorcycle, whipping it around as tourists clutched their hands around him.

She went over and asked if could she get a ride, and he smiled and said, "For you, my dear, no problem."

CHAPTER FOURTEEN

$G$and Randle were staring at the map of the city when G said, "We need to go down around John Hopkins and see what's going on. Most of these groups tend to use college students for cover, and I bet you we will probably pick up on something."

Randle agreed and said, "Let's go," so they jumped into the Altima and off they went.

When they got close to the university, they saw all the students just hanging out by the buildings, all different colors and different nationalities. They got out of the car and started walking toward a group. When they came up on them, they heard them talking about how they felt the university was not doing enough to make the school more affordable. They listened for a few minutes, and then Randle said, "Let's move on. These are rich kids complaining about attending John Hopkins, one of the most expensive schools in America. The fact that they're even enrolled here means somebody has some money."

G said, "You' re right. We need to go back downtown near the Lexington Market or over by the John Hopkins Hospital in the hood; that's where our boys are probably hiding."

They rolled down to the hospital area where they saw the young Black drug boys standing on the corner. As they rolled up slowly, a young teenager approached the car and asked, "Do you want to buy anything?"

G smiled at him, which totally disarmed the young brother. When G said, "No thanks, we're looking for the brothers with suits and bow ties, preaching about righteousness," the young brother said, "Oh, you're looking for the Muslims. They are a couple of blocks down around the corner from Sojourner Douglass College."

As they proceeded, they found the college. It was a big brick building that looked like it had probably been a high school back in the 1950s or 1960s. There was a bunch of men standing in front of another building dressed in suits. Some had on regular ties and some had on bow ties, so G explained to Randle that he had seen the men with the bow ties all his life in Baltimore selling newspapers and bean pies. He never heard anything negative about them, but perhaps they might point them in the direction they needed to go by telling them where the Muslim grocery stores were, which were usually run by foreigners.

Randle looked at G and said, "You are a detective, aren't you?"

G just smiled and said, "I have watched at least 20,000 detective shows on TV. I think I know a little bit."

They got out of the car and approached the men. One of the men said, "Al salam-alakim," and G responded, "Salakim salam."

They embraced, and the man asked, "What can I do for you today? *Final Call* newspaper, Afro American newspaper? or how about a bean pie?"

G said, "I'll have a paper and a pie" and reached into his pocket and pulled out a five dollar bill. While the man was giving him change, he asked where he could get some good meat because his mom wanted to get away from pork and start cooking Muslim style.

The man replied, "You know that market on Pennsylvania Avenue across from the skating rink?" G nodded. "There is a Muslim grocery store in there, and they sell real good beef and lamb prepared the right way."

G thanked him and said he would stop by again in a couple of weeks to get the next paper. The man said, "Cool. Go in peace, my brother."

Randle said, "Wow, that was outstanding, young brother. You are a Baltimorean."

G realized that yes indeed, every fiber of his being was Baltimore and that he was going to find out who and what was being planned.

They rolled out and headed over to Pennsylvania Avenue. As they drove up Pennsylvania Avenue, they crossed Martin Luther King Street and saw the two story projects, and they knew that behind those walls lay the story of Baltimore's working class black folks. They passed the skating rink and on the left they saw the big market and made a left into its parking lot. When they got out of the car and approached the door, an older looking Black man in his sixties asked if they had some change they could spare. Randle reached into his pocket and handed the man a dollar, and he said thank you about fives times and "God bless you."

As they went inside, the market was bustling with people women and men shopping at the cell phone store and the check cashing store, with people playing the lotto and eating at the seven or eight food stands. That's when G saw the little grocery store that said Halel Grocery Store and some Arabic after that. He knew that must be it, so he told Randle, "Let's just hang out here for a few minutes and see what's happening."

Randle walked over to the fruit drink stand and ordered a strawberry drink, and the young lady was very pretty. Randle said, "Hello!" and started a conversation. "Is this fresh?"

She said, "Oh yes, we only use fresh fruit. The strawberries are plump."

Randle laughed and said, "And so they are" as he looked at her hips. She laughed as well.

G went over to the cell phone stand and asked about the cost for a prepaid cell phone. The guy said, "Twenty bucks for the phone and twenty bucks for the activation and first 100 minutes."

G said, "That's a good deal. I'll take one."

The guy grabbed a box and opened it, showing him the phone, and said, "Will this one work for you?"

G said it would while keeping an eye on the entrance to the grocery store. He saw women going in and out for a few minutes, and then he saw several Arab looking guys with neatly trimmed beards walking toward the entrance. They were wearing regular jeans and tee shirts. They looked like they had been in America for awhile, as they spoke to several Black people along the way. G made the assessment just that quickly. He looked over at Randle, who was being handed the drink, walked over to him and said, "I think we're at the right place. After you finish your drink, let's go in and ask for a leg of lamb. Let's say my mom wants to make some shish kebabs."

Randle said, "Sounds good to me. Let me say one more thing to the honey. I'll be right back." Randle walked over and asked the young woman her name. She told him Keon, and Randle said, "That is a nice name. I don't think I have ever met a Keon."

She smiled and said, "That's because I am one of a kind."

Then he asked, "Could I get your telephone number?"

She looked at him hard and said, "Are you a nice guy?"

He said, "Yes, I am," so Keon wrote down her telephone number and handed it to him. G was watching and noted to himself that Randle had the ability to make friends quickly, and that would make them a very good team.

They proceeded into the grocery store. The place was clean and had some soft foreign music on, sounding like European pop music. They made their way around to the meat section, and the meat was behind glass and looked freshly cut with good color. The guy behind the counter asked, "Can I help you?"

Randle said, "We're looking for some lamb. Our mother wants to make some shish kebabs."

The guy smiled and said, "I've got some freshly cut leg of lamb, and I can put it on the sticks for you if you want."

Randle said, "We'll take the lamb as is. Mom likes to put it on sticks and cut up the green peppers and tomatoes herself."

The guy wrapped up the lamb. They walked up front to the counter to pay for it, where a guy was at the register. Randle reached into his pocket and pulled out a twenty dollar bill. G sensed a bit of arrogance in the guy as he looked at the twenty and held it up to the light, checking to see if it were counterfeit.

G did not say a word as Randle said, "It's real."

The fella said, "We just have to check; some people try to pass us phony money sometimes." G headed for the door, and Randle followed him out with the bag.

When they got into the car G asked him, "What do you think?"

Randle said, "I didn't notice anything really out of the ordinary. What about you?"

G said, "Well the first thing that I noticed was that there were no women working there, and to me that's a problem. If you have lived in America any length of time and especially in a Black neighborhood, you try and have women working at the register low cut tops. You know what I mean, unless you are a male chauvinist. And did you notice how the guy at the register looked at us with that arrogant 'I think I'm better than you look', and checking the money? I think that place address and phone number goes on our list and if it pops up again in any reports, we know something's up with them."

Randle said, " I will call the honey up from the fruit stand. That will give me a reason to come by there to see if anything is out of the ordinary."

G smiled and said, "You are a detective," and they both started laughing. They headed back to the office to write up what they had learned and to see what other information may have come in.

As they rode back to the office, a radio bulletin announced that two Baltimore police officers had been shot in Cherry Hill while in undercover status and that details were sketchy.

G thought to himself, "Should we be armed? I will ask the colonel what he thinks, when we see him again." When they got to the office, they checked the incoming reports from the guys in the field. The reports said the word on the street that something was going to happen in the near future, but nothing really hard about who, what, when, or how. Several times Fort McHenry was mentioned. G remembered going there on a school trip while in middle school. It was a very old fort on the edge of the city facing the Chesapeake Bay. There were some very old buildings and a park ranger who gave them a tour and talked about the battle which led to the Star Spangled Banner being written.

G asked Randle if he had ever been to the fort, and he said no, so G said, "Let's go by there tomorrow."

Randle said, "Okay, let's call it a day."

G was ready to go home and just think and chill out, since his mom was off enjoying herself in sunny Jamaica.

CHAPTER FIFTEEN

Achmed walked into his store and spoke to everybody inside, and everybody smiled. They were glad to see him, as it had been a few days. He told them, "I've been to New York; I picked up some more clothes at a good price. Get the stuff out of the truck parked in the back." He then walked into his office and closed the door. He got on the Internet and checked his messages. Nothing but a lot of junk mail, but there was one email with the title "Come and celebrate Defender's Day, The Fort McHenry anniversary with the patriots of today." He noted the time and day 10:00am the following Saturday. He came back into the lobby and asked, "So what's been happening while I've been away?"

"Business has been okay. Some guys had came buy and bought some FuBu stuff. It was on the recommendation from another store on Baltimore Street." Achmed was happy about that. That meant the word was getting around that his store carried some nice stuff. That would keep the doors open. At the end of the day when he counted the money the store had done all right.

Achmed pulled his Taurus 9-millimeter handgun from the drawer and put it on his waist. He had a permit to carry it since he was a business owner. He often went to practice firing with his Lebanese friends out in the suburbs at a gun store named Target in Hanover, Maryland near Fort Meade. This they would do at least once a month. There were four of them, all about the same age, the sons of the older men up in New York City. They had their own businesses in Baltimore–a chicken joint, a gas station, and a grocery store–so they had all grown up together and felt like brothers.

On the way home, Achmed heard a story on the radio about a woman putting her child in the oven and burning him badly before some family relative was able to pull the child out. He thought to himself, "This world is so full of sin that it deserves to burn itself." He promised himself that he would help one day to bring this world to a halt.

When G got home, he checked the mail. There was nothing but junk mail and a bunch of credit card offers. He looked at them and threw them in the trash saying to himself, "Now they want my business." He went into the kitchen fixed himself a couple of ham and cheese sandwiches and sat down in front of the TV, flipping the channels on the remote. Nothing was on but news and ESPN. He watched for about an hour and then took a shower and went to his room.

He noticed on top of his dresser his mother had left him a small Bible, and for some reason he decided to read it, just turning the pages randomly and stopping at Psalm 27. He read it and took it all in, feeling stronger and knowing that he was a soldier dedicated to the protection of his country. Then he did something that he had not done in many years. He actually got on his knees beside his bed and said a prayer, "Oh Lord, give me the strength and wisdom to do this job and to do it well, in Jesus name." Then he jumped under the covers and went to sleep.

G awoke the next morning feeling energized. He did a little stretching and then did forty sit ups, forty push ups, and forty squats. He took a shower, put on his clothes, and was out the door at 6:00am. He stopped at the McDonalds around the corner and ordered a sausage egg McMuffin and a orange juice.

When G got to the work, he decided to take the stairs rather than the elevator and climbed the stairs two at a time. He walked into the section and looked at the big map of Baltimore which had pinpoints on it of addresses or phone numbers that were of interest. He smiled as he saw the clothing store and market he and Randle had been to were now on the map. That really pumped him up some more. G thought, "That means the colonel considers us agents and trusts the information we obtained."

G sat at his desk, turned on his computer, and read the reports from the last week. He looked for a trend or a pattern. Most of it was so sketchy, mentioning small rumors of something big that was supposed to happen, but nobody could say who, when, where, or how. G decided, "I need to know more about this Achmed. That there must be a reason he is connected to this. I will invite the young lady that works at the store out for dinner or lunch to see what I might learn from her."

G then decided to chill out until Randle arrived and run it by him before they talked to the colonel to ask him what they should do next.

All of sudden some people were hollering for everyone to come to the TV room. The news was showing that in Detroit, twenty four gas stations throughout the city had just exploded, causing fires all over the city. People were panicking as the black smoke was billowing everywhere. The news reporter was commenting, "This was terrorism, and it must have been carefully planned and executed. Why didn't the FBI have a handle on something like this?"

Randle walked in and asked, "What's going on?"

G told him, "Take a look at the TV. Stuff is happening, and we don't have a clue."

He was angry. "We're being attacked right here in the homeland, and we don't know by whom, when, where, or how." Those words burned because he knew when they spoke to the colonel, that is exactly what he would say. A few minutes later the reporter on the television said hospitals were reporting that fifty people were dead and at least a hundred more were injured.

The colonel arrived and called everyone into the analytical cell. He had just gotten off the phone with his military counterpart in Detroit, and the colonel there said they had been unable to infiltrate any of the cells in Detroit. They had been monitoring telephone calls and numerous times twenty four candles had been mentioned, so now they know what the twenty four represented. His team was checking the names of the owners of the gas stations and also to see if they were victims in the death count. He also told him that explosives were used to ignite the stations, which added to the explosions along with propane gas tanks.

The colonel looked everyone in the face and said, "We must protect Baltimore from anything like this. Everyone, check the previous two weeks reports and look for anything referring to a number that could be a clue as to how many targets we're dealing with. They are using our own stuff against us. Very clever, that way they don't have to buy any thing in large quantities."

The colonel then told G and Randle to come with him as he walked into his office. "So tell me what you guys have been doing with this Achmed fella."

G then told him about the market and the clothing store and that he had noticed the camera at the clothing store seemed out of place for such an establishment. He also told him his observation that the market had nothing but Arab males working in it in the heart of a Black neighborhood and why he thought that was odd to not have hired a few Black women to work the cash register to keep the customers coming back. He also recounted how the man at the register had an arrogant almost militant demeanor about him.

The colonel sat up in his chair when G said that and said, "You detected that attitude?"

G said yes.

"What about you, Randle? What was the guy's attitude?"

Randle said, "I agree with G's assessment. The guy had that 'I am better than you' body language and look in his eye."

The colonel then said, "I want you guys to go to Captain Johnson. Sign for ten thousand dollars of cash and start spending for information. Talk to the people who hang around at both places and pay them one hundred dollars for any information on anything they see that is strange or suspicious. Tell them you are in the Army, not cops, but that you want to prevent in Baltimore what happened in Detroit this morning. They will understand that you are soldiers and that you are not cops." The colonel smiled at both of them. "Can you do this without blowing your cover?"

G said, "Yes, Sir," as did Randle. G said, "Sir, I was wondering if we are at the point that we should be armed."

The colonel eyebrows raised. He looked at G and said, "American blood has been spilled here at home. We're at that point. Tell Captain Johnson I said to get you both some permits and 9mills for self-defense purposes." They both saluted and then walked out of his office.

G said, "Where is Captain Johnson's office?"

Randle said, "It's upstairs on the top floor," so they walked up the stairs. Captain Johnson's office was actually in a cage-like contraption. It had a big safe in it and a couple of lockers and a desk.

G spoke up first, "Sir, the colonel told us to come to you for ten thousand dollars after this morning's attack in Detroit."

The captain smiled and said, "That's all you need?"

Randle was quick to say, "For now, yes, but if we need more we will be back."

G then said, "Also the colonel said we could have two 9mills for self defense purposes."

The captain smiled again and said, "You guys are about to do it for real. Catch those sons of bitches and make them pay."

G said, "We will do our best" as he picked up the 9mills and a box of ammunition. Randle had the money in a black book bag.

The captain said, "Spend it all. We don't take money back once it's been issued. You can spend it on anything–women, alcohol, apartments, clothes–whatever it takes to get those terrorists."

CHAPTER SIXTEEN

*B*ack in Jamaica, on the television at the hotel, Althea heard the news about the attack in Detroit, and she was concerned that crazy people were just running wild in this world.

They were all eating breakfast. Lisa asked Pam, "How was your late night jet ski ride?"

Pam blushed and smiled at all of them and said, "Let's just say a jet ski is not the only thing he knows how to ride."

They all busted out laughing and said, "Girl, you are something else."

Pam had had a good time, but she knew there was nothing there but a good time, two ships passing in the night with no intention on anything serious, and she was cool with that.

Althea thought to herself, "I could never be that bold, but I do want some romance in life." she wondered if it would ever come her way again. She still loved her dead husband, and she knew it. Althea smiled at her friends and said, "So what's the plan for today?"

Lisa said, "The front desk girl recommends we take the tour bus to the Dunn's River

Falls. She says the water is beautiful as you climb up the rocks with cold Jamaican water pouring down over you. It's only twenty five dollars."

They all agreed to go. As they rode along the coast to the falls, they saw how beautiful Jamaica was. The sun was shining on the Caribbean sea, and people were on the beaches, some swimming, some with fishing rods fishing for dinner. The bus driver was telling everyone about what each little town was known for as they passed them.

When they arrived at the falls, there were about ten other buses there with tourists unloading. A man was giving directions, and a lady was collecting tickets. They had already paid, so they handed her their tickets. She said, "Enjoy the falls. It is a pretty day. When you get to the top, you will feel energized."

They all had on their swimsuits with wraps around their waists. When they came to the bottom where the falls water was splashing down beautifully, they could see a rainbow right before their eyes. There were about five young Jamaican men with them, and the leader said with a smile, "Welcome to the falls, everyone. We will be walking on the stones that are like steps as we go to the top. The water is fine today, but everyone should hold hands as we go up."

They held hands and started walking. Althea could not believe how good the water felt. It was a warm day, about 80 degrees, and the water felt awesome as it splashed all over her. The young men would help people along the way if anyone slipped or had a problem, and of course they were very handsome. She thought, "It must be the weather down here that has caused all of these men to look so handsome." Her girlfriends were laughing and joking as well. She asked Pam, "What do you think?"

Pam said, "I will never forget this. This is fantastic."

When they got to the top, everyone thanked the young guides. They said, "No problem."

On the bus ride back the driver said that the group also did other tours. There was the rum factory, and another place named Trelawney where the fish glowed in the dark at night. It was a very beautiful trip, if they were interested. They told him they would think about it and would let the lady at the front desk know. They stared out the windows at the coconut trees and the sea as they made their way back to Montego Bay.

When the bus driver pulled up to the hotel, they were glad to see it. They went to their rooms, showered, and met for lunch down at the restaurant. They chitchatted about going shopping the next day and then just relaxing before flying back to Baltimore. After lunch Althea went back to her room and just stood on the balcony looking at the people walking along the road, thinking, "I wish John could have seen this place, and we could have been here together."

CHAPTER SEVENTEEN

G and Randle were at the desk looking at the map. G said, "We need to hit the streets with some of this cash and see if it can do some talking. Let's hit the Avenue market again."

Randle said, "What about Fort McHenry? I thought you said it had popped up in a few reports."

G said, "You're right. We will go by there today as well. I just think we need to get that grocery store covered."

Randle said okay, and they started down the steps. G handed the permit and a small card to Randle that stated "U.S. gun permit authorized by the U.S. government," signed by the attorney general. Randle said, "That's all right, we are doing it."

G said, "I'm on a mission, my brother. We will find these guys before they strike. My family is here; failure is unacceptable."

As they pulled into the market parking lot, G saw the old man at the door again. He told Randle, "We will hire this guy for fifty dollars to watch the front of the market for anybody strange that he does not recognize."

Randle said, "Great idea."

G approached the old man and he smiled like he recognized them and said, "Could you gentleman spare some change?"

G said, "Sir, how old are you?"

The man replied, "I'm 55."

"What's your name?"

"My name is Jessie Franklin."

"So, you're old enough to have been in Vietnam?" G queried.

Jessie answered, "I was there in 65-66 in the Army."

G and Randle both smiled and the old man looked at them strangely and said, "Why do you ask?"

G looked at him as seriously as he could, and said Mr. Franklin, "We are in the Army today, and our country was attacked today in Detroit by terrorists. I don't know if you saw that on the TV."

He said, "I saw it on the TV inside the market here."

"Well, Sir, we need your help. We don't want that to happen here in Baltimore. We want you to be a part of the Army again."

He smiled and said, "You must be kidding. My Army days have passed."

G said, "I don't think so. You standing here is like a sentry guarding a post. You see everyone and know who is a regular and who is not correct."

"Yes, that's true."

"Well, we will pay you. How much do you usually make in a day out here?"

"Well, about ten dollars at the most. I'm trying to make it on my social security disability check, but it's not that much after I pay my rent and electric, not much left after that."

G said, "I understand. We will pay you fifty dollars a day for the next couple of weeks to watch who comes here and especially to the grocery store inside, where those foreigners are."

"You know who I'm talking about?" G asked.

Jessie nodded and said, "Yeah, I know. You think they might be involved?"

G said, "We don't know. That's why we want your help. Watch that entrance, and if you see anybody strange with that funny look in their eye, get a tag number and remember what they look like." G handed him a fifty dollar bill and a card with his phone number on it.

The old man straightened his back and said, "Yes, Sir," like he was back in the Army.

Randle said, "Let's go inside." They smiled at the man and walked inside. Randle was looking for the juice girl but did not see her and said, "Damn. It must be her day off. I will give her a call later on today."

G was staring at the market, but he only saw women walking in, so he said, "Let's go over to Baltimore Street and Pratt Street and see if this Achmed is back in town."

On the way over, it was on all the radio stations about the terrorists attack in Detroit and the Black DJ said, "It was a crying shame that they keep letting all these foreigners come here who hate America but won't give a brother who was born and raised here a job, a loan, or anything to get ahead." G understood the frustration in the voice of the DJ. Being black and American was a duality he had read about in high school. W.E.B. Dubois' stories *The Souls of Black Folks* were written way back in 1904 about the duality of being Black and American. It was some deep writing, and as G listened to the DJ, he knew what he was saying when he pondered, "How come all the stores and gas stations have foreigners that own them? And why can't we be businessmen and not just athletes and entertainers?"

After about ten minutes of commentary, though, the DJ was back to playing booty shaking music. It did not seem right, but that was all he knew to do. He had said his peace, and now it was back to "Back That Thang Up" by Juvenile and "Bump 'N Grind" by R. Kelley…"My mind is telling me no, but my body is telling me yes."

G just laughed, and Randle said, "What's funny?"

G said, "Did you here the DJ try to be serious for a minute? Then he follows that up with lyrics by R. Kelly."

Randle started laughing too and said, "That's what were fighting for—the right to be ourselves and enjoy life. Most Black people aren't into killing and hurting other people. Most of them just want to be happy and find real love. The only thing I want after I get out of the Army is a good job, and a good woman."

G said, "I hear you, my brother, same here."

They pulled up on Baltimore Street and saw a crowd of people in front of the stores conversing about the day's events. G was looking for anybody who might help out, and he saw a Black market movie guy who was selling movies. He was a dark-skinned older guy who looked like he was in his late thirties.

G approached, and the guy said, "I have the wolf man movie, the best wolf man movie ever made. He's a stone cold killer." Then he smiled showing his gold teeth.

G and Randle both started laughing with the brother, and then G said, "You are quite a salesman, my brother. Are you down here every day?"

He responded, "Monday through Saturday from ten in the morning till about four thirty."

G moved in closer to him and asked him had he ever been in the service, and he said, "Like the Army or the Marines?"

G said, "Yes, exactly like the Army."

The brother said, "No, I dropped out of high school and could not get in."

So G asked him, "What high school did you go to?"

"Carver."

G said, " I know it well. I went to Dunbar, and now I'm in the Army. Did you hear about what happened in Detroit this morning?"

The brother said, "Yeah, I saw it on the TV."

G said, "Well, we don't want that happening here. Can you do something for me?"

The brother said, "Depends on what it is."

G looked at him as seriously as he could and said, "Brother, I love this city, born and raised here. I got family here, and my girl comes down here to shop on the weekends. I don't want anything to happen to Baltimore. If you see or here anybody talking about blowing something up, we need to know."

G looked at Randle, Randle nodded his head and said, "The Army needs to know because we're stone cold killers when it comes to protecting the home front. You feel me?"

The brother smiled widely as he heard his own words coming back at him. He said, "I hear you, soldier."

G and Randle shook his hand, and G had a hundred dollar bill folded up and placed it in the brother's hand when he shook it. G said they would be around and they walked back to the car. When they got into the car, G looked at Randle and said, "That was right on time, my brother. I think he will be of some help just by the way we explained it to him."

Randle said, "I agree. Where to next?"

G said, "Fort Mc Henry."

They crossed down passed the Inner Harbor over into the Federal Hill area and made a left at the sign that said "Fort McHenry this way." They saw how the neighborhood changed from mostly Black to mostly White, as G explained, "This was where most of the Irish people live." They pulled into the parking lot, got out, and walked into the visitor center. It was pretty nice inside with a lot of old paintings of the fort with information below the paintings describing the events that had occurred there.

The lady at the information desk asked, "Do you want to view the film?"

G said, "Yes, why not?"

They walked into a little theater and took their seats. The curtains in front of the screen were drawn, and everyone stood as the national anthem was played. G remembered this from his childhood visit there, but it caught Randle off guard as he stood and saluted. The film started, and it described how the revolution had started and the people from Maryland who played a part in it, and how Baltimore was an important city. Then it moved on to the war of 1812 and how the British wanted to conquer Baltimore. It described the battle at Fort McHenry and the Star Spangled Banner being written by American Francis Scott Key, who had been captured and taken aboard a British ship. At the end of the movie the Star Spangled Banner came on again, and a park ranger appeared at a door and asked the visitors to please follow him for the tour.

The tour was very educational and the fort very impressive. The thickness of the walls and it shape just made G wonder how they could make such a thing so long ago. As they walked by the cannons facing out toward the Chesapeake Bay, the ranger explained how these cannons had held off the British ships from entering the Inner Harbor and taking Baltimore.

Right at that time a cruise ship was sailing out, and G asked, "Where is it going?"

The ranger said, "Most likely Bermuda."

As people were waving from the deck of the cruise ship at the people on the fort walls, G looked at the ship. It was beautiful and obviously was packed. Then he looked at the long row of cannons pointed directly outward at the ship, thirteen canons to be exact. G smiled to himself and said to Randle, "Let's go."

CHAPTER EIGHTEEN

Achmed walked into his house on Mosher Street near Edmonson Avenue. It was an old wooden house that he and his dad had lived in for almost his entire life. He decided to keep it even though most of his relatives had told him, "Sell it while it still has some value since the neighborhood is getting worse." Crack heads and heroin addicts were everywhere in this neighborhood, known as Edmonson Village, and you literally had to dodge trouble like a dodge ball game, being on the lookout at all times for bullshit happening.

Nobody ever messed with Achmed though. They knew his father. If they were too young to have known his father, when they saw Achmed who was well built at 6'2" about 215 pounds, they would think twice and then decide, "Maybe this is not the guy we want to mess with." His eyes were penetrating, and he had a good smile. The ladies were attracted to him because of his smile, and neat little P Diddy mustache and goatee.

The house was neat and clean on the inside. There was a nice 47 inch television in the living room, a black couch and love chair, and a deep red wall that set off the black furniture. In one of the bedrooms he had a computer hooked up to the Internet. There were two book cases full of books on philosophy, religion, science, and history. His dad had told him, "Study history so that you don't make mistakes that others have already made."

One of his dad's favorite books was *The Invisible Man* by Ralph Ellison. His dad had said it was his favorite book, and he felt related to the main character. Achmed saw the similarities and felt related, too. Some of the other books Achmed had been given as a youngster to read were *The Isis Papers, The West at Bay, Before the Mayflower, Message to the Black Man, The New World Order,* and *I Never Had It Made.* There were many others his father had given him to educate him outside of what the public school system was teaching. Achmed would talk to his dad every weekend about being prepared for the future, getting good grades, and staying out of the clutches of the enemy. These books and what he saw on the mean streets of Baltimore had helped shape his outlook on this world. Achmed thought at its core the world was anti-human and built on greed, jealousy, envy, and power.

A picture of Achmed and his dad was on the table, and he looked at it and thought about his father every day when he would come home. His mom had died when he was a child. He did not have any real memory of her. His father said one day she came home and said she was not feeling well. He took her to the hospital. The doctors ran a bunch of tests, and after several days they told them that she had pancreatic cancer and that it had spread to other organs. They gave her less than six months to live, and she died three months later. Achmed was three years old when this happened, so he and his dad were very tight.

Achmed remembered his father talking about how much he loved his mother and that he would never marry again. He saw other women and had friendships/relationships, but none would ever be called his wife. Achmed respected his dad for that very much and thought, "Will I ever meet a woman that will capture my heart?"

All the women he had met so far were schemers, manipulators, and low self-esteem types, always trying to get into his pocket since he was an entrepreneur. So, he played the game and played it well. He had dated many but never put a ring on any finger yet. His bedroom had a beautiful picture of a Black man embracing a nude Black woman that set the tone for all who entered. He would like to say to the ladies, "See that painting, my dear? That's you and me." And, with a nod of the head, it was R. Kelly in the background: "You remind me of my jeep, and I wanna ride."

Achmed took a quick shower and turned on the TV and saw on the news about the bombing in Detroit. He said to himself, "It's beginning. When am I going to get the chance to make a difference?" In his mind, things needed to change around here. The drugs, the confusion, the crime–it all lay in a society that says, "You can do anything except say you're sorry. And in a few weeks, they let you go and do it again." He was certain that Islam would make a difference. "If this country would turn to Islam, this nation would be better." He had been told this by his father and his father's many friends, and he believed it. He knew he was supposed to meet some more believers on Saturday at Fort McHenry and then maybe they would tell him what the plan was. So, he turned on ESPN, watched a little sports, and then fell off to sleep.

CHAPTER NINETEEN

*A*s Althea packed along with her girlfriends, she thought about all the fun they had while here in Jamaica, and that she would definitely come back again. They all met up in the lobby, and a bus came by to take them to the airport. As they drove back to the airport, Althea took it all in again. There were people walking on the street in their swimsuits and wraps, everyone smiling and talking. She wondered why Baltimore had lost that. She could remember as a child that Baltimore was a happy, fun place to grow up.

When they got to the airport, they were shocked at how long the line seemed. It was longer than the one at BWI. Althea looked at Pam and said, "Wow, this plane must be packed." Pam said, "Everyone returns on the same flights. Don't worry, we have our seats. That's all that matters. This was a great idea. We definitely should take another trip again next year, maybe to another island."

After a few minutes the line started moving, and the next thing they knew they were boarding their plane and heading home. The flight was smooth as Althea stared out the window at the well lit cities down below. As they flew over DC, the pilot said, "We will be landing in Baltimore in about twenty five minutes." Once they landed, got their luggage, and went through customs, they all hugged and went their separate ways.

G was waiting outside his car and was happy to see his mother had made it back safe and sound. He waved to her, "Mom, over here!" As she walked toward him, he gave a her hug, and put her luggage into the trunk. Once she got into the car, he asked her, "So how was it?"

She smiled and said, "It was the best trip I have ever had in my life. The people and the atmosphere were just wonderful."

G smiled and said, " I thought you were going to like it, just like going to Germany and seeing a whole new world."

She said, "You're right. There is a big wide world out there, not just here in Baltimore." G maneuvered up 295 just like his Uncle Bobby had done for him, avoiding the potholes with skill.

Althea asked him, "And what have you been doing while I was gone?"

G told her, "I have been helping the recruiters by going out to different markets and talking to young people about joining the Army."

She smiled and said, "I'm so glad you're not involved in any of this craziness going on. Did you see what happened in Detroit?"

G looked at her and said, "Yeah, I know. They'd better not bring that craziness here. Killing innocent people is unacceptable."

Althea could hear it in her son's voice he was serious, speaking like a real man, that he was not just a spectator but an actor in this life. She looked at him and said, "You are this family protector now."

G said, "Don't worry, Ma. My Army buddies and I will look out for Baltimore, even if the FBI or police don't know what they're doing." G felt a whole lot better that he had told his mother the truth without actually revealing the whole truth.

When they got home, Althea got on the phone and called her sister Ruth to tell her all about the trip. G went upstairs put on some shorts and came back downstairs and turned on the television; it was about 10:15pm. He thought about calling Lakeesha but changed his mind and said to himself, "I'll call her tomorrow." He turned on ESPN and then fell asleep in the chair.

When he woke up the next morning, he did his forty push ups, forty sit-ups, and forty squats, took a shower, put on his clothes, and was out the door by 6:30am. He decided to skip McDonalds today; instead he stopped at a nearby Burger King and ordered a sausage egg, a cheese sandwich, and a small orange juice. When he got to the office, and he sat in front of his computer, turned it on, and started eating. He wanted to review the reports related to the Detroit attack. He wanted to see if he could learn anything from them. As he read them, they detailed that many of the employees at the gas stations that had exploded were dead, not the actual owners of the gas stations. He noted that and thought to himself, "That could mean something or it could mean nothing. All the explosions had happened early in the morning, catching people getting gas as they were headed out to work." He thought that made sense to kill as many people as they could. Several of the reports mentioned that foreigners were so heavy in the Detroit area it was hard to see anything strange since they were all over the city and not just on one side of town. Some of the dead did not have any identifications found on them, so the belief was that they were illegal aliens. The conclusion of the report said all the explosive devices had the same signature and were probably put together by the same bomb maker.

G thought, "That is good to know. Find the bomb maker and stop the attacks."

Right about then Randle walked in and said, "What's up? Is the colonel here yet?"

G said, "Not yet. The secretary said he was at a bunch of meetings and should be in about 10:00am." This gave G a little time to formulate in his mind what he would say to the colonel about the cannons at Fort McHenry. He went on the Internet and downloaded several pictures showing the fort and the cannons.

Randle said, "I have been thinking about why the older guys have not been able to get any information. I just think it has to be some young guys like us that just ain't even associating with no old cats."

G nodded in agreement, "Because they hate America and really are planning to do something, they are not sharing that with anybody outside their little circle. The question is how far along in their plan are they, and can we find out from this Achmed fella. I know in my bones they using the brother."

Right about then the colonel came in, and G and Randle followed him into his office. The colonel looked at his secretary and said, "Tonya, can you bring me some coffee? It's going to be a long day." The colonel sat in his chair looked at both of them and said, "Ok, what do you have?"

G said, "Sir, we went over some old reports going back three and four weeks, and we saw in several of them Fort McHenry had been mentioned, so we decided to go out and take a look. Have you ever been there?"

"No, I haven't been out there yet. It's been on my list of places to see while I am assigned here. What did you find?"

"Well, Sir, we saw the film about how the British wanted to capture Baltimore, but Fort McHenry being at the mouth of the Inner Harbor prevented the British ships from entering and forced them to leave. And, Sir, this was done by thirteen huge cannons that face directly at any ship passing in or out of the harbor. So what does this history lesson mean?"

The colonel looked at both of them and started grinning at his two young protégés. He was thinking these two young soldiers have shown more initiative than some of his older veterans, and he felt good that they both had a defender's spirit.

G said, "Sir, right as the park ranger was telling us about the battle, a cruise ship went right in front of the canons, and people were waving at us from the decks of the ship." The colonel set up straight in his chair as G handed him the photos showing canons and the water. "Right there, Sir, is where the ship passes by. In several of the reports, the number thirteen has been mentioned."

The colonel looked at G and said, "That is some fine reporting, Steen," and stood up and shook both their hands. The colonel then said, "I will contact headquarters and get some ordinance guys to make sure those cannons can't fire under any circumstances. They can do this in the middle of the night so as not to tip off the bad guys. What else do you have on this Achmed guy? Have you met him face to face yet?"

G said, "No, not yet."

The colonel said, "This guy is tied in with that New York crowd somehow. I can feel it in my bones. Get close to him without him noticing. See what he's doing and who he's meeting with. The FBI don't have the agents for this, and the police have their hands full with the regular criminals, so it's up to you two. Report back to me when you have something again. Good job, guys, on the cannons."

G and Randle walked out of the office pumped up. G asked Randle, "What do you think?"

Randle said, "We just hit a home run. Without a doubt when those assholes try and use those cannons, they are probably going to explode in their faces. So, how do we get close to this Achmed guy?"

G said, "We need to go by the store, buy some more stuff. Then I can hook up with that chick and find out what's going on."

Randle said, "Good idea."

G said, "Let's go by there about three o'clock this afternoon, a little too early to be shopping for clothes."

Achmed was at the shop in the back room surfing the Internet and doing some paperwork. His buddies would be dropping by about lunch time since they were going up to security mall for a little get together to chit chat and talk about what had occurred in Detroit. He was anxious to hear about what the plan was and what part he would play, since they had always promised him he would get his chance to live up to his father's reputation among the older men. He always had the feeling that his dad must have done something for the cause since these Lebanonese men respected him so much. His dad had never told him what it was, though maybe they would tell him after he did his own.

Unknown to Achmed, there were men down in Trinidad of Lebanonese descent that cared nothing about him, but they were planning to use him to attack his city where he was born and raised and where his own relatives lived.

Anthony Hawkins, with his English sounding name, was actually a second generation Lebanese immigrant to the sunny island in the Caribbean. He lived in the capital city of Port of Spain and could see the cricket field from his house on the hill and the men in white playing cricket all day long, as though the world were one grand holiday. He hated America and thought that it was the cause of all the problems back in his father's homeland, and he was going to use his chemistry degree to make America think twice about being involved in the Middle East. There were no innocent people as far as he was concerned. He had been told that there were some believers in America that just needed some guidance, and that is what he planned on providing. He had a visa and a plane ticket, American Airlines flight leaving tomorrow for BWI airport. He was looking forward to taking a tour of the city of Baltimore.

Althea went to work and felt totally recharged after her vacation. She was smiling at everybody and told everyone that would listen how much she had enjoyed Jamaica.

CHAPTER TWENTY

*A*bout eleven o'clock, Achmed's buddies pulled up outside his store and blew the horn. He joined them in the big Cadillac Escalade. They headed north on Edmonson Avenue until it turned into Route 40. Mustapha started talking about what the brothers did in Detroit and how they had those police chasing their tails. No one had been arrested so far, which was an excellent sign that if things were done right, nobody would get caught. He looked at everyone in the car, and they all nodded their heads. Khalid said they needed to go out tonight and celebrate.

Achmed said, "Where are you thinking about going?"

Khalid said, "I think we should start off at the titty bar, Eldorado's. Last time I was there, there were some fine honeys."

Achmed said, "That works for me. I need to see for myself." They all started laughing. They reached the security mall, parked, and walked into the food court area. The place was full of people and lots of women were there as they ordered up some grub.

As they were eating, Mustapha said, "We have a brother arriving tomorrow who will give us guidance on what we are to do, my brothers. So be prepared. Get your houses in order. No excuses."

They all nodded. Mustapha was their leader and had all the contacts with people up in New York, and they followed his lead. They decided to stay at the mall for awhile since they had some friends who owned a couple of shops there along with a record store and a jewelry store selling fake gold and silver watches. Achmed had spotted a couple of nice looking honeys at one of the stands selling perfume and oils.

As he approached one, the girls said, "Sir, would you like to try some of our oils? A drop here or there in your car will have it smelling good for days."

Achmed flashed his smile and said, "I can think of a couple of places I would like to put a couple of drops," as he stared at her firm breast.

She smiled as well and said, "We all have dreams, but they don't always come true."

He said, "True that, but ain't nothing wrong with dreaming" as he reached into his pocket and pulled out a wad of cash.

Her eyes got big, but she said, " I know you are not trying to impress me with money."

He said, "Oh no, this is just how I roll. You see, I have my own business as well. I have a little clothing spot down on Pratt Street."

She said, "Oh, really." Now she was impressed because she did not want to be talking with any drug boy.

So he asked her, "What's your name?"

She said, "Karen, nice to meet you. I am Achmed."

As he handed her his business card, she smiled and said, "You are a smooth brother. Is your cell phone number on this card?"

He said, "By the way, yes it is. And I would love to meet you at a club some time. We could do a little dancing, and perhaps you would allow me to buy you a drink."

She started laughing and asked him, "You don't have a girl-friend, do you?"

He said, "No, I do not. Why?"

She said, "Because you are too smooth, my brother, and I know your type. You just want to be friends get the skins, and then move on."

Achmed had heard this before, and his comeback was, "I just have not met the right woman yet. So, I prefer we be friends, and if it turns into something more than that, I'm open to it." He said this with a big grin.

She smiled and said, "Okay, we will hook up somewhere soon. I'll give you a call." Achmed paid for the oil, thanked her, turned around and walked away, confident that he would get that call and eventually get them skins.

On the television at the food court, the news reporter said a U.S. Navy ship overseas had been blown up and several U.S. sailors were dead. The ship was damaged badly. Mustapha looked up and called all the guys over and said, "Stuff is happening all over the place. Stay focused."

They all looked at him like, "What the hell are you talking about? We're here on a pussy hunt, and you're talking about business."

The Arab boys may not want Black people working for them, but they love the sisters. Each of them had several Black women they were dealing with, but under no circumstances would they let their sisters date any Black guys, including Achmed. They liked him like a brother, but just not like a brother-in-law.

CHAPTER TWENTY-ONE

*B*ack at the office Randle was on the phone talking to the juice girl at the market. She was at work and sounded happy to hear his voice. He made small talk by asking how was she doing and if everything was going okay. She said yes, everything was fine, and that complaining would not change anything. She started talking about how her sister was staying with her but was not going fifty-fifty on the bills.

Randle rolled his eyes up into his head and said to himself, "Women are all about money." Fortunately, he had a book bag full of it. Maybe he could help her out a little bit.

When he offered, she bit hard, "Really? You would do that for me?"

Randle said, "I must be honest–being plump just does something to me. It makes me do things I would not normally do" and started laughing. She laughed as well. He said he would try and drop by there about one thirty. She said fine; she'd be there until four o'clock.

He swung around in his chair. G was on his computer, doing research on past attacks in the U.S., and thinking hard about what they needed to do. "We need to find out where Achmed lives, get somebody into his house and see what he's reading, who's sending him mail, who's calling him. We know he's got money since he's got a business and we know he travels, I wonder if he's got more than one gun."

Randle interrupted and said, "Did you hear me on the phone? I have a one thirty appointment with the juice girl; we should leave now."

G nodded his head and said, "Let's roll."

As they pulled into the parking lot, they saw their man at the door. He smiled as he saw them approach. "Hello, gentlemen, how are you two today?"

G said fine, and Randle said, "We're doing all right. How about you?"

The old man leaned forward and said, "I have some information for you."

G perked up and said, "Well, step over here out of the way. We don't need anyone to overhear us."

The old man said, "I saw three of those grocery store guys today, and they are looking more suspicious since the bombing in Detroit. They rode off about an hour ago in a Cadillac Escalade, Maryland tag number 3FM 700."

G said, "That's some good info. How many of them again?"

He said three, and G handed him a fifty dollar bill. "Good job, sir. Keep a lookout for anything else that may look out of the ordinary, delivery trucks that you have never seen here before dropping stuff off to their store, or big boxes, FedEx deliveries or anything out of the ordinary. We'll be back in a couple of days again." G shook his hand and then walked inside, with Randle behind him.

He saw Keon and smiled as he approached. "Hello, my dear, how are you?"

She smiled back and said, "Better now that you are here. You are a man of your word and right on time."

He could tell by her comment she really did need some money; her sister must have let her down. He asked, "How's business been going here?"

She said, "Okay. We sell quite of bit of juice. People are trying to be more healthy and cut back on the soda."

Randle said, "Well, come on down for a minute and give me a hug." She walked around from behind the counter, and he got a chance to see her up close. She was fine, a tight body with very nice hips. He hugged her tightly and whispered in her ear, "I got your back, don't worry" and he slid four one hundred dollar bills into her hand.

She quickly looked at them and whispered, "Thank you." She kissed him on the lips, and said, "You are a good man, I can tell."

Randle was shocked. He liked her for real but was working at the same time, so he said, "I just don't want anything negative to happen to you. My hope is that you are happy and have a good life, if you know what I mean."

She said she did. "Nobody should have to live like some of our people are living with the drugs and diseases that are out here."

He looked her in the eyes and said, "We should get together for dinner or something, like a movie."

Her response was, "I can do that. When?"

He said, "How about tonight? I can pick you up at about 7:00pm. I have to start early because I have to be at work tomorrow about 7:00am. If that's not too early for you, that is. I know how ladies need a little time to get ready."

She said, "No problem; seven is fine" and wrote down her address.

He said, "I will be there and on time. I have to go with my partner for a few minutes. See you later tonight!"

G had walked over to the lottery stand where he could see the entrance of the grocery store and had not seen anybody that caught his attention going in or coming out of the place. He asked Randle how things went.

"Well, we're going out to dinner and a movie tonight."

G smiled, "You are moving right along."

Randle said, "I really do like her. Who knows? She might be the one" and started laughing.

G started laughing as well. "Yeah, right. Let's go check on the clothing store."

They walked out of the market and waved at the old man. He waved back, and they headed downtown. As they drove downtown, they heard on the radio that a city councilman had been shot and killed last night at a club under mysterious conditions. Somebody had said it was a robbery, but no money had been taken from the club, and none of the club employees had been shot. The reporter said further investigation would be required.

G looked at Randle and said, "That doesn't sound right. I have never heard of an elected official being shot in Baltimore. Better bring it up to the colonel. I don't put anything past these killers we're after."

Randle agreed. He asked, "So, G, you got a girl, or are you playing the field?"

G said, "I have a friend down in Tampa, Florida. In fact, I am supposed to be going down there to see her but we have been so busy, I have had to put it off."

Randle looked at him and said, "I don't think you'll be going anywhere soon. You might as well invite her up here and see if she passes the mom test."

"The mom test? What are you talking about?"

"Well, if a woman gets along with your mom, it usually means she will be good for you. No need in having a woman that does not like your mother because as my dad told me in life there may be many wives, but you only have one mother."

G said, "That's deep. My brother, I will have to write that down in my little book. You are right; I will give her call to see if she can come. My mom would like that."

As they pulled up down street from the clothing store, there were several cars parked on the street.

G said, "Let's get all these tag numbers and run them to see if any of these cars are Achmed's."

Randle said, "Good idea."

When they walked into the store, the girl was there, but the guy was not.

"Hello, Lisa, how's business going?"

She said, "Slow so far. You remembered my name!"

"Of course I did. I told you I would be back. I'm looking for a couple of shirts and perhaps a date," he responded with a twinkle in his eye.

She said, "That won't be a problem. The shirts are over here, and when were you thinking about this date?"

"I was hoping tonight, dinner at the Inner Harbor, and then we figure it out from there."

She thought about it for a minute and said yes. He told they should start early because he had to be at work early tomorrow. They decided on 7:00pm, and she wrote down her address for him.

G asked, "Where is everybody? It seems dead in here."

She said, "Everybody's out to lunch or just shamming because they know I will watch the place."

He commented, "It always amazes me how Black business men always end up turning it over to women because they get caught up in the bling, start chasing women, and end up with nothing.

She just smiled and said, "Do you know Achmed? Because when he's with his boys it's all about who can hit it and then keep moving."

G looked her in her eyes and said, "As long as he ain't hitting you, I'm okay," with a big smile.

She returned his smile and said, "I don't mix business with pleasure; that's why I'm here. All the other women that have worked here made that mistake, and after he got tired of them, he let them go."

"Good, I just want that to be understood. If we are going to be friends, I would not want the boss smiling in my face when I drop by here to see you, and he's sticking in the back room on the couch."

She started laughing. "How did you know he had a couch and a small bed in the back?"

G just smiled and said, "They don't call me Baltimore Blue for nothing. I know this city and how the brothers here think. He don't want to bring her to his crib, she might want to move in, so he brings her here after closing time, tags it, and never gives up the crib."

She started laughing and nodding her head in agreement, "I just hope you're not like that brother," she warned as she pointed her finger into his chest.

Randle had walked outside while all this was going on, so G bought a couple of shirts, got her number and address and said, "I will pick you up at seven sharp." He held her hand warmly and walked out.

When he got outside, he smiled at Randle.

Randle said, What's up?"

G told him, "I learned a lot just from that short conversation. The old boy has a back room with a couch and bed for hitting his honeys because he does not want them to see his house. As soon as we get the tag number run and come up with an address, we need to see inside his house for some clues."

Randle said, "That's a plan," as they drove back to the office. Once they ran the tag numbers and an analyst brought them the results: Achmed Jackson on Mosher Street, silver Q45 Infiniti.

Chapter Twenty-one

G said, "That's a nice car, a honey magnet."

Randle started laughing and said, "I agree. You roll up in that, and she will at least listen to what you have to say."

They wrote the information down and put in a request for a discreet house search. G added in the memo request that he and Randle be allowed to come along. Since they were so involved in the case they might notice something that the searchers might overlook. This would take a few days to get an answer. In the meanwhile they both had dates for the night and called it quits to go home and get ready.

During the time they were out, the colonel had met with a working group with the FBI and Baltimore police department on preventing an attack like that which had occurred in Detroit. The FBI was in the lead, and the agent told everyone present that they didn't have any good leads and no good informants in any of the suspected groups that might be involved in terrorism. The colonel took notes and listened intently.

The Baltimore police detective stood up and said that they didn't have any informants on any group that was talking about blowing anything up. He said they were noticing an influx of heroin into the city that was coming from central Asia. Most of their informants said the stuff was coming from boats in southern Maryland, and the city of Benedict was the jumping off point. It had many places along the coast of the Chesapeake Bay where small boats could sneak heroin or illegal immigrants into Maryland. He said they also had heard that Bladenburg, Maryland was where a turf war was happening with most of the drug dealers targeting Washington D.C. at first, and that now they were marching up toward Baltimore.

The colonel then stood up and said that the military was using all its resources to find, fix, and then kill these terrorists. He had appointed a Major Samuel Smith to handle the protection of Fort McHenry, which had been identified as a potential target. He told them he had a couple of young agents that were trying to infiltrate these groups and to find out what they were planning. He told them that he understood that they were primarily crime fighters, but that this was war without uniforms and that if they heard anything, even the smallest clue, to please pass it on to his office so that they might connect the dots.

Everyone nodded their heads and stood up and said, "We are with you, Colonel. If you need anything from us, let us know."

CHAPTER TWENTY-TWO

*R*andle was right on time at Keon's place, and it did not look like a bad apartment complex from the outside. She came out and was looking good with some nice fitting jeans and a pretty top. He said, "So hello, and how are you?"

"I'm fine, and I wanted you to know how much I appreciated that money."

"No problem, I told you I got your back. What kind of food do you like?"

"I like sea food," she responded. Down at the inner harbor were some nice restaurants, so they headed down Route 40 to Green Street then down to Pratt Street and over to the harbor. Randle found a place to park, and they walked over to the pavilion.

Keon said, "The Cheesecake Factory has good food."

Randle smiled, "That's fine. I'm with you—you're from here, so show me the ropes."

She smiled back and asked him why he had joined the army. He told her he had joined because he wanted to see the world and learn a trade so he could have a career and not just a job.

She asked, "Are you going to stay in the army, or are you going to go back home, and where is home?"

He told her, "I'm from Lanett Alabama, a little small town on the Alabama/Georgia state line about 85 miles from Atlanta. It used to have a lot of textiles mills, but they have all closed down, so now everybody grows up and moves to Atlanta." He told her how he wanted to have a family one day, and to be happy is what he really wanted, but that he was doing his time serving his country right now.

She told him she was glad they had met, how she liked what he stood for, and that she could tell he was a man, and not a boy trying be a man like so many she saw every day with their pants hanging down and just wasting their lives.

Their food arrived and it looked so good on the plate, Randle wished he had a camera to take a picture of it. He said, "Wow, look at that! It's almost too pretty to eat." After the food was gone he asked her why she didn't have a boyfriend right now.

She said candidly, "Because he wanted to play games, get high, and not do anything for real, so I let him go."

Randle could tell she was a good woman but needed a good man, so he said, "I want to ask you in all honesty, do you like me, and could you see us hanging out on a regular basis?"

She looked him in the eyes and said, "I could see that if it means that you would be honest with me and not just be interested in my plump hips but be interested in my mind."

"What can I say to that? You know I like your plump hips, and I do want to know what's on your mind, so lets be friends for awhile before we do anything so that you know for sure that it is you I like and not just your body." With that she smiled, leaned across the table, and kissed him softly on the lips. They paid the check went to the movies and had a good time.

When he dropped her off at home, she hugged him and said, "Call me when you get a break tomorrow."

He said, "I will. Sweet dreams."

CHAPTER TWENTY-THREE

G pulled up outside Lisa's apartment and said to himself this looks like a *Good Times* complex with all the kids' toys that were outside; Big Wheels were everywhere. G smiled and said to himself, "Lots of babies up in here."

As Lisa came outside, she was looking good in some tight pants that showed her form, and she was well endowed.

"Hello, my dear, how are you?"

She said, "Fine, now that you are here."

He looked at her. "You didn't think I was coming, that I was going to call at the last minute and say I couldn't make it."

"Yep, that's what usually happens when I meet a nice guy. That or he's already taken."

"I feel you, my sister, but not all of us good guys are like that. Some of us are single men, and we don't have anyone special yet. I am one of those good guys. I'm focusing on my career and having some fun because I'm still young. Are you cool with fun, or does everything have to be its leading to something long term?"

She looked at him and could see he was serious. He was young and sure of himself. She could see that his being in the army had made him more of an honest and upfront guy, not the scheming, conniving, hustling brother that she was used to encountering. She started laughing, "Yeah, G, I'm okay with fun, just as long as it does not lead to a broken heart."

He looked at her and said, "Lisa, I will not do that, I give you my word. So tell me, what do you have a taste for?"

They headed down Edmonson Avenue toward the harbor. "Phillips Seafood works for me; I like those crab legs that they have there."

G said, "That works for me as well. They have a nice buffet. I heard you can try a little bit of everything." As they drove down Edmonson, he asked how the rest of her day went. She said all right; nothing eventful happened.

"So, did the boss make an appearance, or was it one of those four hour lunches?"

"You got it," she said. "He didn't get back until about 5:00pm just as I was locking up."

He laughed. "Like I said, some brothers get a business just for the perks–women, clothes, jewelry–and to be seen, not really to make the business a great success."

She said, "You are a mind reader, but when someone gives you the business, I think people don't appreciate it like the original owner."

"Oh, so someone gave him the business?"

"Yeah, his dad passed away and he got it from there."

"Oh, I understand now. That makes even more sense. When I get my own business, I'm going to be there because it's mine."

She had to ask, "What type of business are you going to open?"

"I am going to do imports and exports, mostly imported bottled water and sodas from the islands. Everybody is going on vacations these days. Jamaica is hot," he said with a big smile.

"People are taking cruises right from here in Baltimore, and my plan is to bring back a little sunshine in the form of water and sodas from the islands. You feel me?"

She smiled and said, "I feel you, my brother, but that is going to take some cash, isn't it? Is the army paying like that?"

He smiled at her and said, "I have saved a little bit of cash since I've been in. The bank account is not skinny and is headed toward being fat." They both started laughing. He felt good to be able to talk with a home girl who understood exactly what he was talking about. Then he threw in the kicker, "I will be needing a business savvy sister to run things for me, if you know what I mean."

She smiled back and said, "I know what you mean, G."

As they pulled into the parking lot at the Galleria and walked across the street to the pavilion where the Phillips restaurant was, they ordered the buffet, loaded up their plates, and laughed and joked about the city, discussing things they remembered about growing up in the city. After dinner they walked to the movie theatre, saw a flick, and just had a real good time.

He dropped her off in front of her apartment, and as he leaned forward kissed her on the lips, he told her, "I will call or drop by tomorrow if that's cool with you."

She looked at him and said, "Fun, right? Not leading to something else?"

He nodded. "Right, baby, I'm all about fun, no drama."

When he got home, his mom was in the living room watching television. She asked him how his day was.

He told her, "It was a good day. We are really doing some interesting stuff, and I am learning a lot about what it really makes this world operate like it does. You know, Ma, I never really thought about it as a kid just growing up how all of this stuff is here, food everywhere, street lights, running water, hospitals, schools, roads, airplanes, trains…and that you can be anything you want to be if you study and go after it."

She just smiled at him and said, "I am glad that your eyes are so open now as to what you can do instead of focusing on what you can't. My parents had it much harder than me with all the segregation back then, but son you have the opportunity to be anything you want if you just apply yourself. You can do it!"

He gave her a hug and said, "Oh yeah, I have a friend of mine down in Florida that I met in Bosnia. I was thinking about inviting her up here for a few days since I'm busy here at work and can't get away. Is that okay with you?"

She smiled again and said it was okay. "What's her name?"

"Lakeesha."

"And do you like her, or do you really like her?"

He looked at his mom and said, "I really like her and thought she should meet you. I still have friends here, but not in the same way, if you know what I mean."

His mother looked at him and said, "I know what you mean, but just be careful. Don't be breaking no girl's heart. Remember, women are more emotional than men."

G said, "I'll be careful" and then went upstairs, took a shower, jotted down some notes of what he had learned that day, and went to sleep."

CHAPTER TWENTY-FOUR

*M*ustapha got up early the next morning. Anthony Hawkins would be arriving at noon, and he wanted everything to be right, so he took the car to the car wash on North Avenue across the street from the Everyone's Place bookstore, famous for selling Black consciousness, Black history books. Everybody who worked there had either been to the motherland or the Caribbean, and Mustapha would get his tapes there. They sold the tapes of the most charismatic speakers of today, and even some of the old Malcolm X, stuff too.

Anthony had requested to stay in a hotel down on the harbor front for the first two weeks of his stay, and initially Mustapha was upset that the brother would not be staying at his place. But, after thinking about it for a while, he realized the brother must have his reasons for wanting to stay in a hotel overlooking the harbor for an entire two weeks. He would not question anything he wanted because this guy was the one they had been waiting on, the one they had been told so many times that one day a brother would come that would help them to make a difference for the brotherhood.

As the plane approached BWI, they flew right over Washington DC, and on the left he could see the U.S. Capitol and the Washington Monument and the Lincoln Memorial all lined up in perfect symmetry. He said to himself, "The capital of the beast is before me. Before it is all said and done, I will make them scream for mercy."

When the plane landed and he proceeded down the hall toward the immigration booths, he saw four men in civilian clothes staring at everyone as they walked by. He thought they must be immigration looking for drug smugglers or illegals. He was not worried one bit; he had his visa as a college student, and all his papers were in order.

When his turn came, he stepped forward. The guy looked at his passport, which had the U.S. visa attached inside the F1 student visa, and the guy looked him in the eye and asked him what school he would be attending.

He responded, "The University of Baltimore." When asked what he was studying, he said, "Business, and then hopefully I will get my MBA from there as well."

The officer nodded his head and said, "That's a good school. Many of their graduates go on to do great things. Welcome to the United States of America."

Anthony thanked him, picked up his passport, and retrieved his luggage. He showed another guard a form that said he was not bringing a large amount of money into the country. The guy looked at him hard and asked if he any cigars. Then he asked if he had any fruit or plants. When he said no, the guy stamped his forms and told him to go ahead.

When he walked through the doors, there was Mustapha with a sign that said "A. Hawkins." He lifted his hand and nodded to Mustapha and said, "Hello, brother. I am Anthony Hawkins, at your service" and started laughing.

Mustapha smiled and said, "Glad to meet you, Sir Anthony" and started laughing as well. They both were laughing at the fact that they knew the authorities would always be on the look out for a guy named Mustapha, but never an Anthony Hawkins.

As they loaded up the Escalade and headed out of the airport, Mustapha said, "I'm glad you made it here safe and sound."

Looking straight ahead, Anthony said, "There were no problems because all of my paperwork is in order. I have friends who assisted with my obtaining a slot at the University of Baltimore, and the tuition has already been paid. All I have to do is register in the next few days, and classes don't start for a couple of weeks, so we have the time we need to prepare and execute." As he turned and looked directly into Mustapha's eyes, he asked, "Are you ready?"

Mustapha smiled. At long last they would be doing something and not just talking. "I am ready, my brother. You lead, and I will follow."

Mustapha guided the Escalade up the parkway and asked Anthony about what Trinidad was like, and Anthony told him it was on the southern end of all the Caribbean islands not very far from Venezuela, about thirty-five miles. He said that the island was a paradise when the original Carib Indians lived there, but since its discovery and conquest by the infidels it has been a living hell for the people living there–the Africans and Indians from India trapped by poverty while the landowners ruled the island with their hotels where the rich from Britain and Canada vacationed.

He told him that his family had migrated to the island back in the sixties from Lebanon, selling diamonds, gold chains, and other jewelry and that the Muslim community was growing. They had tried to take over the government back in the seventies when they saw the country going down and lawlessness was taking over. His older brother had been killed by the British soldiers that were brought in to retake the Red House, the capitol building of the island. He would never forget that they had shot him down like a dog.

Mustapha now understood why this brother was involved and started telling him why he was all for making a mark: "This country America is sick, and only fire will make it straighten up."

As he turned off the parkway onto Pratt Street, they drove by all the big office buildings. Anthony said, "They can build big buildings, but they can't build good people."

They pulled into the parking lot of the Marriott on Alcieana and Fleet Streets. It was a beautiful hotel overlooking the Inner Harbor. Anthony checked in using a visa card the brothers had given him back in Trinidad. He had a forty thousand dollar limit, on it so he felt like that would be more than enough. If not, he was told that the brothers had money coming in from heroin from Lebanon by boat through the huge harbor here in Baltimore. He didn't care; anybody who uses drugs deserves to die as far as he was concerned. He got his room key, and they both took the elevator up to the fifty-second floor. When they walked into the room, the blinds were open, and the view of the inner harbor was spectacular.

Mustapha said, "Wow, what a view, my brother! You can see it all from right here."

Anthony said, "Yeah, and right over there is the famous Fort McHenry where we will make our statement to the world. I want to meet with the rest of the guys tonight for dinner, and will go by Fort McHenry tomorrow where there will be others there as well. I will go enroll for my classes on Monday. Can you find me an old car to use? I prefer not to rent a car to use for the couple of weeks of my stay."

Mustapha nodded his head. "No problem. I know a junk yard dealer who has old usable cars. We will throw a dealer's tag on it and nobody will bother you; the police only stop young Black brothers driving nice new cars in the hood." They both started laughing.

Chapter Twenty-four

Anthony said, "Profiling."

Mustapha said, "Yes, you know it; the devil cannot believe a young brother should have a BMW."

Anthony said, "By the way, we will have to practice somewhere. Do you have a place picked out?"

Mustapha said, "Yes, there are some warehouses over on Cherry Hill overlooking the Pautuxent River that a brother owns. He says he will give me the key and we can use it. That's his contribution to the cause."

Anthony just smiled. "So he's a believer but not a doer?"

"Yeah, that's what he is." Anthony looked out the window again, scanning the landscape. He said to himself, "Yes, I will make these people beg for mercy."

CHAPTER TWENTY-FIVE

*A*lthea went to work that morning feeling good. She was going to call Tony and see what he was doing. She had thought about G bringing his friend over to the house for a visit, and it made her think about Tony. She had not spoken to him since her trip to Jamaica, so as soon she got a break she dialed his number. When he answered, she said, "How have you been doing?"

He said, "Okay. Business has been good. I thought you had forgotten my number!"

She laughed. "No, I didn't forget it, and I should have called you sooner."

"So, tell me about your trip. Last time we spoke, you said you and your girls were going to Jamaica."

"Oh, it was beautiful! The people, the scenery, the beaches..."

"So, did you get in your bathing suit?" he asked.

She said, "Yes I did. The water was so blue–I have never seen anything so pretty!"

Tony had to ask, "So did you get your groove back while you were there?" and started laughing.

She laughed as well, "Oh no, my girlfriends did, but I just could not bring myself to make love with a strange man even though the men down there are very handsome."

Tony said, "I'm glad to hear that. You deserve a good man in your life, someone who appreciates you. You know you are welcome to come and see me whenever you want to…."

She told him, "I will be coming over soon, I promise. I've got to go; talk to you soon."

CHAPTER TWENTY-SIX

*C*olonel Briley and Major Smith were driving down the parkway south to the Pentagon. They were going to brief the general on their progress. The colonel and the general knew each other from way back when they were captains. The general's name was name Danny Louis, and he knew intelligence backwards and forwards.

As the colonel started his briefing, he told everyone in the room that Baltimore had been targeted and that every effort was being made to prevent an attack like what had happened in Detroit. He laid it out about Fort McHenry being used to target cruise ships passing directly by the fort and how it would be very symbolic that the cannons that saved the nation from destruction during the war of 1812, would be used to sink a cruise ship, killing hundreds perhaps thousands of Americans trapped on the lower decks.

The general chewed on a fat cigar and took it all in. He asked the colonel what he recommended.

The colonel said, "I recommend we a get a special forces unit to Fort McHenry. Ordinance guys have already made the cannons unusable, and Major Smith has guys assigned dressed as park rangers on the inside. We need special forces on standby in the houses in the neighborhood that can be on scene in five minutes or less."

The general jotted down notes. Then he asked, "Do we know when they will do this?"

The colonel spoke up and said, "In my professional opinion no later than one month after the Detroit attack, another city will be hit. Maybe Baltimore is next or maybe New York, or DC. I think Detroit was hit first due its closeness to the Canadian border, and the perpetrators fled across the border. I have guys watching the airport and the port for any suspicious persons coming from known threat countries. I have a couple of young agents working our strongest lead, and they are doing a good job."

The general looked at everyone in the room and said, "I want my staff to give Colonel Briley whatever support he needs–no red tape. Colonel, I want you to get some people on the cruise ship staff as waiters or security staff types to search every corner of the ships. Sometimes these guys fake you out with an outside attack when they really are planning and internal attack as back-up. It's my understanding that a lot of the guys working on those ships are from all over the world."

The colonel said, "Got it, Sir, it will be done."

Everyone stood up as the general left the meeting. Staff officers approached the colonel and offered their help...whatever you need sir, boats, planes...the SF guys will be here tomorrow... I am going to make the call right now....

As the colonel left the Pentagon, he felt good. The briefing had been effective. The general had probably left to talk to the chief of staff of the Army. Fort McHenry was a national treasure, and everybody in the army knew what it stood for.

On the drive back, the colonel told Major Smith, "The general was right about checking the ships from top to bottom and the crew; I had not thought about that."

He laughed, and Smith asked him, "What's funny?"

"The general has always been a smart man, just cut out for intell!"

CHAPTER TWENTY-SEVEN

G was at his desk early that morning and writing his report on what he had learned from the previous night. Randle came in and asked when he got there.

"About seven. I figured I'd knock out this report and get it out of the way."

Randle said, "So, how did it go?"

G gave him all the details about Achmed inheriting the business and his plan on getting into the back room after a few more visits. Randle said he would check on the tag number from the market and would swing by the market and get eyes down on the white Escalade.

"Sounds good," said G.

Randle went over to the analyst's desk and asked if he had the Escalade's information, and a young private said, "Yes we do, Sergeant. It belongs to a Mustapha Hamsho, 3133 Riggs Street, Baltimore."

Randle said, "Mustapha, huh? Put that name and address on the map so we can see where it is."

The private went up to the big map of the city, looked up the street, and then stuck a pin in it on Riggs Street. It was not very far from Mosher Street where Achmed lived. Randle nodded his head and said, "They're homeys from the same neighborhood."

G looked at the map and saw where the white Escalade was entered and thought the same thing. "So, they're neighborhood buddies. Probably grew up together in a tight-knit group, and that's why nobody can get inside. We need to take a ride and see what we can see around that way.

"Good idea. Let's roll."

They pulled out of the parking lot and jumped on Monroe Street north to Route 40 west for about five miles. As they entered the neighborhood, G told Randle, "This is known as the Edmonson Village area, a very rough part of town. Brothers leave here dead every other night. It's survival of the fittest , everybody selling crack or heroin."

Randle said, "Damn. Do people really live in these houses? They look like they're about to fall down."

"I know," said G. "They're living hard over here, my brother. If a guy makes it out of here, it is an accomplishment."

Randle said, "The girls are looking fly, shapely with the tight leotards on. Did I just see a camel toe?"

"Yeah, you did, my brother." They were showing the goodies with a shirt barely hanging over the booty, and the leotard with no panties on up under it. "The only problem is– Baltimore has a very high HIV rate with all the brothers going in and out of jail and using needles to shoot up heroin, so I'm telling you, you got to ask your honey did she have a boyfriend who was going to jail. If so, you got to ask if she's been tested–straight up you have to ask."

Randle said, "Good looking out. I'm shocked; the three honeys we just drove by were all fine."

G said, "I know. We have some of the finest women in the country without a doubt; you just got to be safe. This is the type of neighborhood you can hide in. No FBI agent can come here; even the undercover Baltimore police find it hard in here. All these guys grew up together. The ones who decide to become cops are told they have to move from this neighborhood. The department won't allow them to stay because they will be compromised. The drug pushers are serious about their money."

Randle gave him directions to Riggs Street. Half of the houses were boarded up, but 3133 looked pretty good. "So he's taken care of a house in the heart of the ghetto," G said out loud. "He's got money and living well in the hood."

Randle nodded in agreement. "These guys are the ones. We got to get thcm."

G said, "We will, I guarantee you."

Just then on the radio the announcer said a Black man in Atlanta had taken a gun from a sheriff while he was in the court house and that he had shot the judge, a couple of lawyers, and two sheriffs and was on the loose. He was from Baltimore.

Randle looked at G and said, "What the hell is going on?"

G said, "I don't know. These brothers can be treacherous when pushed to the brink. Obviously he did not want to go to prison. It's a jungle mentality. Right then the DJ said something about Baltimore producing some vicious people, and then put on Master P, talking about some booty. G started laughing again, "See what I mean? Five minutes of death and destruction followed up by forty-five minutes straight of booty shaking."

Even Randle had to chuckle. "Yeah, I see what you mean. Let's keep it from happening to us; I don't want to be a five minute episode on the radio."

G nodded his head, "Let it be them that they speak of and not us."

As they drove down Poplar Grove, they saw a group of old men standing on the corner. They decided to go over and talk with them. They were in their class B uniforms and looked sharp as they approached.

"Good morning, gentleman," G said. "We're looking for some potential recruits for Uncle Sam."

All the old men started laughing and responded that their army days had long passed.

G stuck out his hand and shook the four men's hands, "Sergeant Steen. Pleased to meet you. We are recruiters from downtown and are on the look out for talent."

One of the men said, "You're going to be hard pressed to find some qualifying brothers down here; they all have records by the age of eighteen or don't have the high school diploma."

G said, "We can work on high school diplomas, and as long as it's not a felony we can work with misdemeanors." The men smiled at G because of the confidence he was exuding. With a winning smile, he told them he was a Dunbar graduate from the Greenmount area, and with a strong mother and encouragement from his uncle he was able to finish school and now he was serving my country, and defending Baltimore. They all chuckled.

Randle was taking it all in. he was amazed at G's ability to communicate ideas and paint a picture with words.

G then said, "Here is our card. If you have a nephew or a grandson who may be interested in doing something positive and making a difference, give him our number and we will see what can be done." G then looked them dead in the eyes and said, "If you ever see any of those guys with that crazy look in their eyes like they want to blow something up like Detroit, give us a call on that too. We're here to defend home. As he puffed out his chest and clenched his fist, it was clear that the pushups he had been doing been lately were working. You could see his frame was filling out.

The man smiled and said, "We hear you, Sarge. If we see any of those nut jobs, we will give you a call. The police around here ain't doing nothing but harassing honest people, and the drug pushers are selling poison like its going out of style."

G shook all their hands again and then walked with Randle up the street to Mosher Street. A bunch of beat up looking houses and cars were parked very tightly together. "Umm," he thought to himself. "A strange car will definitely be noticed on this street. Everybody has that one spot for their own car in front of their house, and looks like only two visitor parking spaces here at the end of the corner." Randle asked him what he was thinking, and he told him, "There ain't no way for a strange car to be around here for long without being noticed. All these cars are for people who live on this street, so surveillance from around here is out. If it's going to be done, it will have to be from where we work."

Randle looked down the street and saw exactly what G was talking about. A strange face would be noticed as well.

G stated, "I'm thinking Achmed lives right down this street, and Mustapha lives two blocks away. How much you want to bet the rest of his little posse lives in this same neighborhood? Also the old man referred to nut jobs as though he had seen the type of men we were referring to. He did not ask what they looked like; he knew what I what talking about because he has seen them around. You know what I mean?"

Randle thought about it for a minute and recounted the conversation with the old men in his head, and then it clicked that yes in fact they had affirmed they knew what he was talking about because they have seen the types before.

The Baltimore police detectives that had been assigned to help the colonel's task force had planned on catching someone during a traffic stop who was acting suspiciously. They had put out an all-points bulletin to the department that if someone was stopped and was a foreigner and their paperwork was not right to write down the address they were using and a full description of what they looked like. So far they had not received any hits. Most of their drug informants did not have any information other than more pure drugs were coming in from central Asia, and the price was going down.

G said, "Now that we know where they live, we need to find out where they play. There is a recreation center not far from here where the fellas shoot hoops over on Hilton Parkway."

Randle said, "Cool. Let's go check it out."

As they approached Hilton Parkway they saw the rec center, a big building with about eight basketball courts outside of it. There were about fifty to sixty young guys playing basketball and another hundred standing around their cars and the courts watching.

Randle said, "Wow. Ain't nobody working? Everybody's shooting hoops."

G looked at the crowd and then at Randle and said, "I bet you everyone of them is a high school dropout and this is their job, shooting hoops, hustling, stealing, stickup boys...you name it, but a regular job is not the answer. Look for an Infinity or white Escalade as we walk through."

G walked with his head up, and several brothers nodded as G said, 'What's up?"

"Nothing, my brother."

G found a table to sit on, and Randle stood beside it. Randle said, "Just look at all these young Black men. This is bigger than the detachment we are assigned to!"

G agreed. "There is a lot of talent out here, and if had not been for my mom and Uncle Bobby, I would be right here as well shooting hoops. Don't get me wrong; Baltimore has produced some good ballers from this very court–Reggie Lewis, David Wingate–but they were exceptional. Most of these brothers are good, just not focused on other things in life. They took a wrong turn somewhere and ended up being twenty with no hope other than a hustle, having several honeys and a nice car. That's about as big as the dream gets."

Randle said, "I don't see any silver Infiniti or white Escalade. They must play a different game or play somewhere else."

G agreed. "They probably are so intent on their plan, they don't have time to hang with these kind of brothers. Where do you think we should look?"

Randle said, "We need to check out the owner of the Escalade and see if we can tie the two together in any way, and then we will have confirmed the grocery store guy with our clothing store guy. We need to get their driver's license pictures from the Baltimore police and show it to our man at the market to see if he recognizes Achmed being there and getting into the Escalade."

G said, "That's a good idea. Let's roll back to the office and submit that request."

"That works for me."

CHAPTER TWENTY-EIGHT

*A*chmed was pretty excited he would be having dinner with the one who had been sent to put him into action in a couple of hours, so he made a quick stop by the shop and asked Lisa how things were going.

She said, "Fine, nothing unusual. Business is slow, but it's early in the day and I expect more people will be in about 3:00."

He told her, "Great, handle things. I'll be out and about. I have some things I need to take care of."

Lisa said, "Okay, I got it."

Achmed went into the back room, opened up the safe, and grabbed about a thousand dollars just in case they went some place expensive for dinner. Maybe the brother would want to hit the strip club after dinner. They had a good time at Eldorado's the other night and going back there might be a nice introduction to the states for their visitor.

Mustapha went home to get cleaned up for the festivities later that evening. It was a beautiful day in his mind. He was thoroughly impressed by Anthony. He was a good-looking, strong Muslim, and he could tell he knew his stuff. He dialed up his fellas and said they were to meet at his house and drive from there to pick up Anthony and then take him to dinner. He thought that new steakhouse down on the waterfront would be nice. He went upstairs and up in the attic he had a suitcase with about a hundred thousand dollars. He grabbed five all crisp, five hundred dollar bills. His dad had given him the money about two years ago. He did not ask where his father had gotten it, and his father just looked at him and said the brothers had provided it for their use to support the cause.

Achmed pulled up dressed all in white, looking sharp, and the other two, Khalid and Ishmail, were dressed sharply as well.

"Brothers, our moment has arrived. All I can say is, let's do it!"

They all nodded in agreement as they drove downtown to the hotel. Achmed said, "He's at a nice hotel. What's up with that?"

"Mustapha said the room has a great view of the harbor and Fort McHenry from way up on the fiftieth floor, and he said he was only going to stay there for a week or two at the most," Khalid responded.

Achmed nodded, "That makes sense."

When they got there, Anthony was in the lobby sitting comfortably in a chair just people watching as they were going and coming. Everybody seemed oblivious to him as though he were just a piece of furniture. He knew they did not see him; he would have to be a big spender to get some attention, and that he would not do. He wanted to blend in. Mustapha walked in with three other brothers. He greeted them all and shook their hands and gave them hugs, saying, "Pleased to meet you, my brothers."

When they got into the car, he told them they would be spending a lot of time together, so they should clear their schedules and tell no one what they were doing. They should make it about work, buying clothes, groceries, and it would require trips to New York and DC. They all said okay, that they would do as he asked.

Mustapha told them, "I'd rather we talk business while in the car while driving rather than talking business at the restaurant or clubs."

Anthony looked at him in surprise, "We are going to a club?"

Mustapha said, "Yeah, we have just the place."

Anthony smiled a big grin and said someone had lied and said that religious brothers did not like women.

"Well, that's not true. The next best thing to paradise is a beautiful woman!"

When they got to the restaurant, Mustapha talked to the maitre de and got them a nice table. They talked about Trinidad the most. As they peppered him with questions about the island, he told them about Port of Spain, the capitol city, and its many beaches and hills, and some of the most beautiful women in the world. He invited them to visit, and he would hook them up. They all started laughing.

When the food arrived, the plates and the food were sizzling, and the waiter said to be careful. After dinner they headed over to Eldorados, and the parking lot was only half full.

Achmed said, "This is good; we should be able to get a booth." Then he whispered into several of the girls ears, telling them that Anthony was there friend from out of town, and would they please treat him special as he slipped them three crisp hundred dollar bills, and the show was on. They were all drinking Hennessey and just had a good old time. After several hours of drinks and lap dancing, Anthony said he was ready to go. They had an event at Fort McHenry at noon tomorrow. They took him back to his hotel shook his hand and dropped him off.

Mustapha on the way back to his house thanked everyone for showing Anthony a good time, and that he was ready to do whatever it took. "See you all tomorrow at Fort McHenry, 12:00pm sharp."

When Anthony got into his room, he took a quick shower and went straight to sleep. He wanted to be energized tomorrow.

CHAPTER TWENTY-NINE

*W*hen G and Randle made it back to the office, they wrote up the request for the driver's license photos. An analyst told them that there was a reenactment going on at Fort McHenry the next day with folks dressed up like the War of 1812.

G said, "Thanks for the info. We will go and see if our targets are there, so get me those driver's license photos ASAP." G went back to his desk when the telephone rang. It was his mom.

She said, "I have some bad news. Your grandmother passed away today."

G just looked at the phone. He knew his grandmother had been sick, but he did not expect to ever hear that she was not here. His grandmother Lois, his momma's momma, had always been a very religious woman who went to same church, Burnette Baptist Church, the church of an everlasting fire. He remembered sitting by her side in church as a boy and listening to her sing along with the choir. She had been the one who nicknamed him G, and he had been called that within his family his whole life. To everyone else he was Gregory, but to his family he was G.

Althea told him they were working on funeral arrangements and that his grandfather was feeling down. Would he go by and visit him when he got off today? She gave him the address.

He asked, "How are you doing with this, Mom?"

She said, "Okay. I knew she was not doing well, and I expected this day was coming, but I'll be fine. I'll see you at the house. Expect a lot of family to be there."

G said okay and hung up the phone. He swung around in his chair and told Randle, "My grandmother just died today. I need to go see my grandfather. I will meet you here 0700 hours tomorrow in casual clothes."

Randle said, "Sorry for your loss, G. Go ahead and go, man. I will handle everything. See you tomorrow."

G drove over to the assisted living center over by the Lyric Opera House. The building was a tall high rise, and it had a guard desk. G had been over there a couple of times to visit his grandparents, and they both seemed to have liked the place. His Aunt Melody was always visiting and taking things over to Grandma, and seeing to it that she was comfortable.

His grandfather, Carl Steen, had grown up during a different time. Born back in 1930s, he had told G about the many jobs and things he had done in his life to survive here in America. As a young man he had tried being a professional boxer, and at about 6'4" 220, he had the body for it. He won a few and of course lost a few. Then he had been a camera man at clubs and had worked in the horse stables at Pimlico race track and served as deacon in the church.

G got off the elevator and knocked on the door. When his grandfather opened the door, he could see the pain on his face as he said, "She's gone; she's with the Lord now...no pain, no sorrow now."

G's eyes welled up in tears as he thought about his grandmother and looked at the chair where he last remembered seeing her, smiling as she saw him with his uniform on. He asked his grandfather if there was anything he could do.

His grandfather just looked at him and said, "Keep on being a good man. She always loved that about you, and I do too." With that, they shook hands as they always had done since G had been a little boy. His grandfather had always had a very strong grip, as he had used it with all his uncles to show who was the strongest. G could feel the grip was not as strong as it had been, and he knew his grandfather was truly becoming an old man. But, he still had a smile, and G smiled in return.

"See you soon, Granddad," G said as he left.

G drove home. His mother was already there, and the house was full with relatives he had had not seen in years. He spoke with them briefly and then went to his room and laid on his bed. His head was hurting, and his heart was aching. He kept wiping the tears from his face. A big knot was in his throat as he was trying to contain his feelings. He remembered one time when he was in the first grade, and he had gotten lost on the way home from school. Back then there was no bus to school. His grandmother had called the police when he had not arrived at his normal 12:30pm, and they had found him about five blocks away walking in the wrong direction. He vividly remembered the look on her face when they brought him to the door as she gave him a big hug and asked him what happened. All he could say was, "I got lost, Grandma, so I just kept walking."

Althea walked into the room and asked, "G, are you okay?"

"Yeah, I'm okay, just missing her already."

Althea said, "Don't worry; it's just a natural part of life to live, grow up, pick a trade, meet someone, get married, have children, watch them grow up, and one day go to your final rest. It's when you know you have lived a good life, loved the Lord, and loved those around you that you're not afraid of death. She was ready. So wash your face, think about all the good things in her life, and come on downstairs and be with your family."

G got up, went to the bathroom, turned on the hot water, and grabbed a face rag. After he soaked it really well and wiped away the tears from his face, he looked in the mirror and said to himself, "Grandma, I won't let you down."

G went downstairs and started hugging and talking with his cousins Shonnie, Mickey, Rasheem, Tiki, Tashi, Ann, Junior, and Robin. His Aunts Melody and Geri were there, and his Uncle Bobby showed up. They started talking about family. G told him about the handshake with his granddad, and how he could feel he was not as strong as he had been before.

Bobby told him, "G, you are the man of this family now. All the others have tried and stumbled in some way. You could be the one. All of your cousins look up to you, and you are setting a good example for them—no drugs, no alcohol; no scheming and conniving."

G asked Bobby, "Why me?"

Bobby looked at him and said, "Because you are the one—no rhyme, no reason, G. You're just an honest person, a man of character."

With that said, G gave everyone hugs and announced he had a big day tomorrow and that he did not mean to be rude, but he had to get some sleep. They all nodded in understanding. He was a disciplined soldier.

The women told Althea, "Your boy has grown up to be a handsome man, and so well spoken! He looks just like John."

Althea handled the rest of the night. They cooked up some collards greens, fried fish, and macaroni and cheese. They talked and laughed about their childhood days and broke out the old photo albums, looking at the old pictures.

G slept a deep sleep that night and awoke about 6:00am. He rolled out of bed, did his usual routine, and put on some shorts, a tee shirt, and an Orioles baseball cap. He went straight to work and jumped on his computer to check the news to see what had happened overnight around the world. Nothing unusual was on the screen, so he decided to go over all the previous reports from the last two weeks again. Nothing jumped from the pages. Everything pointed to Fort McHenry. He remembered one of his instructors back at Fort Huachuca had told him about being careful of deception.

Randle walked in and said, "Good morning. What's up?"

G told him everything was fine. "It looks like the funeral will be Friday, giving my out-of-town relatives a little time to get here."

The colonel walked in and told everybody to come into the map room. He said, "Today, gentlemen, there is a reenactment happening at Fort McHenry. We will have the place fully covered in case they try and take it over. If not, I believe they will show up to conduct reconnaissance, so we will have cameramen there taking pictures of everyone. The SF guys will be on alert and ready if something goes down."

The colonel then spoke with G and Randle and told them, "Be cool out there today. I want you to see whatever they see. Look at the place from the perspective of a prospective terrorist."

G said, "Yes, sir," and Randle did the same.

When they went back to their desks, the analyst walked up with Achmed's and Mustapha's driver license photos. They looked at them good and locked them in their memories, grabbed a couple of cameras, and out the door they went. When they started getting close to the fort, it was already getting crowded. Hundreds of people were walking toward the fort. Some were dressed up in 1812 outfits and others were in shorts and tee shirts, so G felt appropriately dressed. Randle had on some jeans and a University of Tennessee tee shirt.

When they got to the entrance, there was a park ranger welcoming people and giving them information. It was about 9:00am, and the literature said the event would start at 10:00am and run through 5:00pm. There would be lectures in a lecture tent that had been set up and reenactments. G was especially interested in seeing this. Were they going to use the cannons for the reenactment? Randle was checking everything out. He had never seen any reenactments down in Alabama; it was just not done around where he lived.

It was a beautiful day, about seventy degrees and not a cloud in the sky. There were food stands around selling hotdogs, snow cones, frosty drinks, cotton candy, pretzels, and of course crab cakes. To G it had the state fair feel to it. Everybody was in a good mood. There were stands selling War of 1812, memorabilia, buttons, caps, shirts that said Fort McHenry, the Star Spangled Banner and other neat stuff.

G had lived in Baltimore all his life and was aware of the Fort, but this was the first time he had seen this many Baltimoreans in a patriotic mood. This was not about sports. Everybody loved the Maryland basketball team, but who would think several thousand people would show for this?

He was walking around and had not seen Achmed's or Mustapha's faces yet, so he looked at the set up. There were soldiers running around with muskets and men standing around the cannons. They had poles with which to stuff something into the cannons. Unknown to G, the cannons could still shoot blanks. The ordinance guys had to allow that since this event had been planned prior to any knowledge of the fort being targeted. G watched the men as they practiced loading the blank round. It took about five minutes, and then they unloaded it. They did this twice and then went away.

Randle noticed the ammunition was stored was a small block building. The door was open to the public, so he walked in. There were little round wooden barrels marked "gunpowder." He picked one of them up. It was pretty heavy. He thought to himself, they must have dirt or sand in them; no way would it be gunpowder. He walked outside and looked around for G but did not see him, so he decided to get up on the fort wall to have a better view. From there he saw G over by the food stands and climbed down and walked over.

CHAPTER THIRTY

Anthony woke up early that morning, said his prayers, and then did a few exercises while looking out the window at the view of the harbor. He took a shower and decided to go downstairs for breakfast. He did not want anyone coming to his room unnecessarily. He sat down in the restaurant, and CNN was on, broadcasting typical news stories–murders, car accidents, oil spills. He took notice of the oil spill in the Gulf of Mexico. He saw that it was far away from Trinidad but felt that it must be stopped before it reaches its beaches.

He flipped on the cell phone Mustapha had given him the night before and called him. "Good morning, brother. How are you doing?"

Mustapha said, "Fine. I had a good time last night, but I slept well."

"Good," said Anthony. "Pick me up at 11:30am at the front of the hotel. I will be ready."

Mustapha said, "No problem."

After finishing his cereal and fruit, Anthony paid his bill and walked over to the gift store. A young lady was inside. He asked her where the post cards were, and she pointed to a stand over in the corner. He started going through the post cards and saw one that had the inner harbor on it and the water was reflecting the buildings perfectly. He grabbed two of them and walked to the counter to pay for them. Anthony asked her did she also have stamps.

She smiled at him and said, "Yes. How many do you need?"

He said, "Give me six." He paid for them said thank you and walked out of the gift store.

The lobby was bustling with tourists, and he got on the elevator back to his room. Upon entering the room, he looked at it carefully looking to see if anything was out of place. He sat down at the desk and filled out the post cards. He wrote, "Everything here is okay. You should see it for yourself soon. I will see you in about three weeks" and addressed it to Larry Hitchcock, Port of Spain, Trinidad and the other to Oliver Magellan, Georgetown, Guyana. He put three stamps on each post card and dropped them in the mailbox in the lobby as he waited for Mustapha.

Right on time Mustapha pulled up with Khalid, Ishmail, and Achmed. They all smiled and said good morning.

As Anthony jumped in the front passenger seat, he spoke without turning around. "Did everyone get a good night sleep?" They all said yes. He then said, "I need all of you to start getting in better physical shape...pushups sit-ups, and a little weightlifting. You need to be able to handle fifty to a hundred pounds easily. Is that understood?" They all said yes again.

He then began to talk to them about what to do at the fort that day. "I want you to walk around the entire thing and then get a good look at the cannons. When the reenactments are going on, watch what they do to load and fire those cannons. Also, I have been told there is an impediment to our movement here in this city. The brothers want us to take care of while we are here." He turned around and looked at them and continued, "And take care of him we will." They all nodded. "While on the fort, be happy, smiling, and enjoy yourselves."

CHAPTER THIRTY-ONE

As they pulled up to the fort, the SF guys who were on the scene reported over their radios that the white Escalde was parking in the visitors parking lot. This information was relayed back to Colonel Briley as he was sitting in the analytical cell, listening to the radio calls, and watching the closed circuit television, which was installed on the fort during last few days at the order of Major Smith. They watched as the five guys got out of the Escalade and walked toward the entrance. Once they got inside, two guys dressed in civilian clothes approached the Escalade, inserted a master key, opened the door, and took a quick look around. They did not see anything unusual, but they noted the mileage and checked the glove compartment. There was nothing inside of it but the registration and proof of insurance. They were out just that fast, and back at the house they had rented called the colonel with the information they had.

The analyst walked up to the colonel, did a half salute, and said, "We can confirm two of the guys as being Mustapha Hamsho and Achmed Jackson. We're analyzing the photo of the other three."

The colonel said, "Good, get me the names of the other three. I want to know everything we got on these birds."

Anthony told his guys to split up into twos, and he would walk around by himself for about an hour, and then they would meet back up over by the food stands. They all nodded and went their separate ways. Achmed and Mustapha were together while Khalid was with Ishmail. They followed instructions by walking around the fort at first and then climbed the wall to see it from the top. While Achmed and Mustapha were on the wall overlooking the harbor, Achmed looked at the inner harbor skyline and told Mustapha, "We're going to make them pay."

Mustapha laughed and said, "Keep it light and friendly, my brother. We're going to make history."

At that moment Randle nudged G. They looked up at the wall where they saw Mustapha and Achmed, looking out over the water. G nodded his head and said to Randle, "Gotcha, connection confirmed. Lay back and watch. We don't have to get close. We're still going by the shop and grocery store later, so let's not get close at all."

Randle nodded and ordered a strawberry snow cone, and the young girl asked, "Will that be a single or a double?"

Anthony walked around playing the interested tourist role, reading the information literature which had a map of the fort on it, laying out everything as it was during the war. He watched the park rangers as they were discussing the different areas of the fort. He then ducked inside the lecture tent where an old white-haired man was discussing his book about how if the fort had been lost, America would have become a colony again. Anthony listened about how the politicians of DC had been bickering so much, they had failed to properly defend DC, and the White House was burned to the ground. Anthony smiled as he heard that.

Ishmail and Khalid did their job and checked out the ammunition room. They saw the barrels and picked them up to feel the heaviness of them, and then they understood why they would have to get stronger. After an hour had passed, they met up by the food stand. Anthony said the reenactment was about to begin, so they should watch carefully.

As they moved over toward the rampart where the cannons were located, a guy was reading a journal discussing the battle and then the Americans engaged the enemy as the re-enactors moved with precision loading the cannons. Then, boom! boom! The thirteen cannons fired in succession. The people applauded and stood and cheered. The Star Spangled Banner was played as soldiers ran to and fro, yelling out commands. It was very exciting. At the end, the guy playing the commander thanked everyone for coming out, stated that there would be book signings, maps, posters on sale in the gift shop, and God Bless America.

G and Randle had watched them as they had all come together, and G had noticed the foreign Arab-looking guy doing all of the talking while they were huddled together. He saw them watching the canon procedures intently and would put all of this into his report as soon as he and Randle got back into the office.

Anthony gave the sign to his fellas that he had seen enough. They made their way back to the Escalade and drove away.

Colonel Briley was in the ops cell being briefed about the Escalade's departure, and he started asking questions about Mustapha, and whether or not the camera guys had gotten good photos of the two unidentified men. "I want their names as quick as you can get them. See if you can get some surveillance around their business establishments, but not around their houses. G recommended that approach not be taken, and I agree. I want to see where these birds go after they leave work."

The analysts all nodded their heads and said, "Yes, sir, we will run the photos as soon as they get here."

The colonel's cell phone rang; it was the SF commander calling from the house near Fort McHenry. He said, "My men say they were definitely sizing up the base for some type of attack. They walked around it completely, and it looks like they went into the ammunition building and were in there for a while, probably inspecting the barrels that have the simulated gunpowder in them."

The colonel smiled and said, "That means they are probably planning on replacing replacing some of those with some that have the real thing. Make sure you get a small camera in there and mark those barrels with ultra violet markers."

The captain said, "Yes sir, will do."

The colonel hung up his cell phone and went to his desk phone and called the Pentagon to give his report.

G and Randle got in the Altima and headed toward downtown back toward the office. G told Randle, "I'm psyched we know who they are, where they work, and where they live. Now we have to find out what they are planning and how they will carry out the plan."

Randle started laughing and said, "You really did learn something when you were out in Arizona."

G smiled and said, "I guess I did."

When they got back to the office, they reported what they had seen to the analysts. The analyst were excited. They were working on some good stuff and could talk to Randle and G face-to-face.

The number one analyst said, "You guys are on it. Keep going. What should you do next?"

G looked at him and asked, "Is that a trick question?"

The analyst smiled and said, "No, it's supposed to cause you think about something you may not have thought about before."

G said, "Okay, help me out. What else might we be doing?"

The analyst liked G's attitude and open mind. He said, "You might try and nail down what passes by the fort. Those cannons are too heavy to move, so the target has to pass by it. We have all assumed it is a cruise ship. What other types of ships pass by there, and who would know that?"

G said, "The portmaster would know. How about getting the Baltimore police to get that info? I want to stick on Achmed and what he's doing."

The analyst said, "Fine. I will type up the request, and you will sign it. Only agents can make those types of requests." G's eyebrows went up ever so slightly. The analyst noticed it and said, "Yeah, you two are agents."

G sat down at his desk and thought for a minute. Maybe the analyst was right. It might not be a cruise ship. He jumped on the Internet and looked up ships visiting the Baltimore harbor. A list of ships popped up talking about the foreign military ship visit program, ships from Great Britain, Norway, Brazil, Spain, and Australia were due to visit the harbor in the next few weeks and months.

G thought to himself, "Wouldn't it be ironic if those cannons that had defended the U.S. from Great Britain back in 1812 would be used again to sink a British ship?"

CHAPTER THIRTY-TWO

Althea was over at Melody's house. They were talking about their mom and how she had lived and struggled all her life but kept her sense of humor. Althea said, "Thank you for visiting and taking care of Mom. We were all so busy with our own lives, I think many of us did not appreciate her enough."

Althea was referring to her other brothers and sisters, and Melody said, "It was never a problem or a burden; it was my way of paying her back for being understanding and giving unconditional love. I will always love that about Mom."

Right then their brother Mike walked in and asked if there was anything he could do. They said just be ready to be a pallbearer. Melody asked him what he had been doing lately.

He said, "I've been working as a truck driver delivering furniture and construction equipment." He smiled and said, "No drugs, and I'm looking for a good woman."

Melody's eyebrows raised as she said, "You ought to be looking for a woman period, to put up with your mess!" They all started laughing.

Althea then said she was going to the grocery store and then home to cook for G. Mike asked and how was G doing with the army, and she replied, "He's doing very well. They have him working with the recruiters and doing all types of stuff. I can tell he's doing some good stuff; he's so serious now."

Mike just smiled and remembered his days in the army. He said, "I wish I could have done it differently. It's only afterwards that I realized the army is a great institution." He smiled at them and added, "But who wants to be institutionalized?" They all laughed again.

Althea got into her car and drove to the Food Lion grocery store near her house. When she got there, there was a fire truck and an ambulance outside with the sirens going. She walked inside, and there was a crowd of people standing around watching an older lady being put on a stretcher. She asked a lady what happened, and the woman said a crazy man had walked into the store and just started punching people. He hit the woman in the face and knocked her out.

Althea was shocked. "What is going on? My neighborhood is losing its mind." She picked out a few items and paid for them. She asked the lady at the register, "Has this ever happened before?"

The young Black girl said, "No, but I'm not surprised. We need some security around here. There are no guards, mostly just women and a few men in the back who cut meat. Drugs, drugs, and more drugs. He was either a crack head, or on heroin, or crystal meth. They got these brothers so strung out, it's a crying shame."

When Althea got home and turned the lock, she felt better. She thought that was somebody's momma laid out on the floor, just shopping and trying to feed her family. She knew if that had been her, G would probably search the entire neighborhood and put a hurting on him. She tried not to think about it and turned on the television. Law and Order was on. She quickly changed the channel to Who Wants to Be a Millionaire and watched it while the food was cooking.

CHAPTER THIRTY-THREE

As Anthony rode with the guys, he asked them what they had learned. They started telling him about the ammunition building and the heaviness of the barrels. He asked, "How many pounds would you say they were?"

Khalid said, "About fifty at least, maybe more."

"What about the procedures for loading the canons? Do we have a handle on that?"

Everybody said yes. "Put the powder bag in first, then push the cannon ball end, and light the fuse. It looked pretty simple," said Mustapha.

Anthony agreed. "But the timing is what is important. The ship will be in front of the cannons for about five minutes at the most, so we must have the cannons loaded and be ready to move from one to another methodically. It is still a beautiful day. Can you show me the national aquarium you have here in Baltimore? I have heard its beautiful."

Achmed spoke up and said, "Yes, it's right next to the Baltimore world trade center building. If we go to the top you can see the entire city."

Anthony said, "Good. I would like to go there, too." He then said that there was a ambassador from Trinidad down in DC who had played a part in the government crackdown on the Muslim brother hood back in Trinidad, and the brothers wanted him taken care of. They all listened intently as he turned around and told Achmed, "We want you to do it. You can move around in DC and no one will notice. The Hindu must be dealt with."

Achmed nodded his head, "Tell me when and where, and I will do it."

Anthony said, "We have his address, northwest DC. We have a delivery man uniform and a van. You'll pretend to be delivering a package Monday. Be ready."

Achmed nodded his head. Everyone was quiet in the Escalade for a minute as they digested what had been said and realized that Anthony was not joking around. Achmed started thinking about what this Hindu must have done to fellow believers back in Trinidad that they wanted him dead, and that he had been selected to do the deed. He knew they were testing him to see if he was like his father, a true believer. Well, he would show them.

When they got downtown to the aquarium, there were families and couples walking around holding hands. They paid fifteen dollars each entry and went inside. It was spectacular– the biggest fish tanks in the country with thousands of fish. The tour guide said they have tried to acquire at least two of every kind of fish in the world, and that it is hard because some fish don't like each other and have to be separated or they will kill each other.

Anthony turned and looked at them and said, "Some fish just don't belong" and started laughing. They all laughed and finished the tour and walked to the next building, the trade center, paid the ten dollar fee, and took the elevator to the top floor. When they stepped out, the room was one huge window through which you can see the entire city of Baltimore. Achmed had never been up there, so he was shocked at how clearly one could see. He looked at Cherry Hill and then over at the fort. At the mouth of the harbor he saw the small white boats going out and coming in.

Anthony said, "See, the ship will be right in front. They come right over here down below by the restaurants to the dock."

They then swung around to the other side where Mustapha pointed out the warehouse where they would practice. Anthony said, "Good. Close, but not too close. I like it. Take me to a computer café joint. You do have them, don't you?"

Mustapha said, "Yes, we do. They're always around the colleges. I know one over by John Hopkins."

Anthony laughed. "Yes, I know John Hopkins. I think he was a friend of the original Anthony Hawkins."

CHAPTER THIRTY-FOUR

When G and Randle decided to call it a day, G went home and called Lakeesha down in Florida. Luckily, she was home and answered. He asked her, "How was your day?"

She said fine, and then he told her that his grandmother had passed away and that the funeral was on Saturday. He was wondering if she could come.

She was shocked. "Do you want me to come?"

G said, "Yes. I have been thinking a lot about you lately, and I want you to meet my mother. I have told her all about you, and she is looking forward to meeting you."

Laskesha thought about it for a minute and said to herself, "G must be for real if he wants me to come to his grandmother's funeral and to meet his mother during this difficult time," so she said, "Yes, when do you want me to come?"

G smiled and said, "Tomorrow. I need you to call the airport, arrange a flight that will land after five in the afternoon, get the price, make the reservation, and I will drive out to the airport here and pay for the ticket."

She was excited now and said, "Okay, I will do that right now and will call you back in thirty minutes." They hung up.

G went downstairs where Althea was in the kitchen cooking and said, "Mom, she will be here tomorrow."

Altheas said, "Who will be here?"

"Lakeesha, my friend in Florida. I invited her to come for Grandma's funeral and to meet you."

She looked at him. "That girl must be special if you're bringing her here for the funeral."

He nodded, "Yeah, I like a her lot. When we talk on the phone, it's like she standing right here and I feel like she is on my side, not out to hurt me or get over on me. You know what I mean."

Althea said she did. "What time will she be here?"

G said, "After five. She's making the reservations now, so I will drive out to the airport and pay for the ticket tonight."

Althea asked him, "Isn't that going to be expensive?"

G said he had some money from his time in Bosnia he had kept, so it was not a problem and she was worth it. Right then the phone rang; it was Lakeesha sounding very happy. She told him Southwest Airlines flight 1920 arriving at 6:00pm, and it cost $500.00 since it was so late.

G said, "No problem. I expected it would be that much. I got you. The reservation is in your name?"

"Yes."

"I'm on it. I am going to pay for it right now and will call you when I get back from the airport."

He ran upstairs and to his closet. He pushed open the little door and felt around for his backpack from Bosnia, and he counted out six hundred dollars just in case there was taxes on the ticket she did not mention. He still had about three thousand dollars left over from his time in Bosnia and Germany. He had not spent it all on his car. He jumped in his car and rolled out onto to 295 South and was at the airport in about twenty minutes. He found a place to park and went inside to the Southwest counter. A young Black lady was behind the counter in her early twenties. He explained he was paying for the roundtrip ticket for Lakeesha from Tampa to Baltimore arriving tomorrow.

She looked it up and said, "Yes, flight 1920 arriving at six pm tomorrow with an open window of thirty days for the return. That will be five hundred and thirty-nine dollars; thirty-nine is the taxes and fees."

G just smiled and handed her the six hundred dollars. Right then his cell phone rang. It was Lisa. She said, "What's up? I thought you were coming by the shop to see me today."

G was caught off guard just a little. "I got tied up at work, and we were not able to swing by, but I will definitely be by there tomorrow. What's a good time for you?"

She said, "About one, let that time crowd come and go."

"Sure, no problem," he said. "I'm at the airport right now taking care of some arrangements. I will call you back in the morning, okay?"

She said, "Okay, handle your business," and hung up.

The girl behind the counter looked at him curiously and said, "Girlfriend number one..." as she looked at copy of the ticket and "girlfriend number two on the phone...which one has your heart?

G smiled and said, "One is a friend, and one is my girlfriend, and I'm here buying my girlfriend her ticket to come see me and to meet my mother."

As she handed him his receipt, the girl smiled and said, "Well, she must really have your heart for you to introduce her to your mother. Good luck."

G walked away and thought to himself, "Things are getting complicated. I need to figure this out. So do I tell Lakeesha what I'm doing and what I may have to do for my country?"

He drove back home and called her up and told her the ticket was paid for and he would be there tomorrow to pick her up. She was very excited and told G how happy she was to be coming to Baltimore to meet his mom and his family. Her mother had said it was a good thing, too. G said his goodbyes until tomorrow and went into the kitchen got his plate and joined his mom in the living room.

Althea was excited about Lakeesha's visit and told him, "Don't worry; everything will go well."

G ate his food and told her, "I have a busy day tomorrow, so I am going to turn in now."

CHAPTER THIRTY-FIVE

*A*nthony walked into the café, ordered up a couple cups of tea, for himself and Mustapha, and then sat down at the table with the computer on it. He wrote a short little message to an email address located in Detroit saying that the business was good and everything should be sold in the next few weeks. After that he started talking to Mustapha about growing up on the island, where everybody had to wear school uniforms, different colors for each grade. He looked at Mustapha and said were about to graduate from school very soon.

After they finished the tea, they headed back to the hotel. Anthony told Musatpha to keep up with Achmed until Monday when they would take care of the Hindu down in DC. Mustapha said no problem and let him out in front of the hotel. When he got home, he turned on the television and watched a little ESPN. He was wondering why Anthony was concerned about Achmed. Didn't he trust him? He didn't know why, but he was sure Achmed would come through and then everything would be fine.

Achmed was at home just thinking that in a day or two he would prove that he was a real brother willing to go all the way and defend the cause. His father would be proud knowing that he had stood up and done something about all this evil going on around him.

The next morning Anthony called Mustapha and asked him to go for a ride. Mustapha picked him up in front of the hotel and asked, "Where to?"

Anthony said, "DC, near the zoo."

Mustapha sped down 295 to 495 to the Wisconsin Avenue exit. He told Anthony this was the nice side of DC; Southeast is where all the trouble was.

As they approached the zoo, Anthony looked at a photo he had of the streets, and he pointed to right passed the zoo on the left on Winthrop Street. They turned and drove down it to about the middle of the block to a big brown house with a nice looking front yard. Anthony told him to slow down get a good look at that house. "That's where the Hindu lives."

There was a blue BMW and a white Mercedes in the driveway. Mustapha got a good look.

Anthony said, "Okay, let's go back, but take me by the White House first. I would like to see it for myself."

As they drove down Wisconsin Avenue, Anthony told Mustapha that others had scouted the house earlier and had given him the picture, but that he wanted to see it for himself and that he wanted Mustapha to see it, since he would be driving Achmed tomorrow.

Mustapha smiled and said, "You are like a maestro at a symphony, using all of the instruments to make beautiful music."

Anthony said, "Tomorrow I want you to go to a cleaners over in Park Heights. Some brothers of ours will have a freshly cleaned delivery man uniform precisely Achmed's size," as he handed him a cleaner's ticket.

Mustapha then realized that Anthony had other helpers in the Baltimore DC area, folks he had never met, but it was all good as long as everybody was doing their part. As they approached Pennsylvania Avenue they could see the Capitol building. They made a right turn onto Pennsylvania Avenue and drove down a beautiful street lined with government office buildings. When they got to where the White House was, they had to swing around to the Washington Monument side, where they saw the side of the White House that is always in the movies.

Anthony said, "One day there will be a direct attack on this house."

Mustapha asked, "How will it happen?"

Anthony said, "It will be simple. They give a lot of parties there. Just get on the list and walk in with a beautiful woman on your arm like you belong." Then he started laughing.

Mustapha started laughing, too. "Let me check the list–oh, here you go. Your names are right here; come on in and have some food and some liquor and meet the president."

Mustapha pointed the car toward southeast, and they went through Anacostia rather quickly as Mustapha pointed out what look like a war zone of abandoned cars, houses with broken windows, refrigerators in the front yards.

Anthony said, "Wow. It looks like another planet, and only fifteen minutes from the White House. These devils need to go."

When they got back to the hotel, Anthony said, "Don't forget to check on Achmed today. Keep his spirits up."

Mustapha said, "No problem. I will hook up with him in about an hour."

CHAPTER THIRTY-SIX

*G*got up early and went into the office to see if anything new had come up. There was nothing out of the ordinary, so he gave Lisa a call. She answered sounding half asleep. "Hey, it's me, G. What you doing?"

"I'm half asleep. I went out last night to the 347 Club and danced the night away."

G said, "The 347 Club? I haven't heard about that one."

She said, "Because it's a new club behind Mercy Hospital on Calvert Street."

G said, "Really? And what type of music do they play?"

Lisa said, "It's house music all night long, nonstop. You have to be prepared to dance because they ain't slowing down for you."

"Sounds like my kind of place. Do you want to go to breakfast?"

She said, "Yeah, you picking me up?"

"Yes, I'm on my way. Be there in about twenty minutes."

She jumped up and ran into the bathroom, and took a quick shower. She found a tee shirt and some jeans, put them on, and then turned on the TV. A church program was on, New Psalmist Church, and the pastor was preaching about love, and the power of love. It sounded good, but she felt like she had never had her love returned in the same way, so she guarded her heart.

After a few minutes G pulled up outside, and she rushed out the door.

G said, "Hello, my darling."

She looked at him. "Do you say that to all the women in your life or just me?"

G said, "Of course I say it to all the women in my life. You are in my life, right?" and started laughing.

She said, "Yeah, I'm in your life. So tell me, where are we going for breakfast?"

G said, "Let's try the Golden Corral out in Glen Burnie. I need to stop at the Lowes Store while we're out there and pick up some stuff for the house that my mom wants."

She said, "Okay, that sounds good."

G jumped on 695, and they were out of the city and in Glen Burnie in about twenty minutes. While standing in line G was face to face with Lisa asking her about her dance moves. She moved her body up next to his and said, "I was working it last night."

G just smiled and said, "I'm going to need to see this for myself."

She said, "Certainly. If you had come by yesterday, I would have told you about the 347 Club, and we could have met there. I would not have been with my girlfriends talking about nothing but men problems, trying to have a good time."

"Oh, I see you have a little posse of friends, and it's all about the brothers."

"Yeah, that's right."

"When it's all said and done, it's about relationships, right?"

She nodded her head, "Yeah, really, that's it."

G paid for their food. They grabbed a tray, found a table, and went up to the food bar. They were both a little hungry and got some bacon and eggs. G got some grits. He had started to like them after being in South Carolina. They talked for a while and laughed a lot at the different looking people in the place, fat and small, tall and short. G cracked a couple of funny jokes, and soon Lisa was laughing so hard tears were coming to her eyes.

After a while, he said, "We should go before we end up in a fight with one of these fat people."

She said, "You're right," so they left a tip, got into the car, and drove a few blocks over to the Lowes. They went in and got a few light bulbs, some hooks for paintings, some scrubbing bubbles for the bathroom, and a couple of filters for the furnace. He told her his mom had given him a list of things; otherwise, he would have forgotten half of this stuff, but it was all good.

She said, "You are a good son, I can tell. Don't change; just keep being you even when the cool people try to make you change."

He drove her back to her place, and she invited him in, so he came in. It was a decent looking apartment on the inside, and it was clean. He noticed that and asked her, "You're very neat aren't you?"

She smiled and said, "Yes I am. I would not have asked you up if it was all junkie."

G sat on the couch. Lisa came over and sat next to him and asked, "So, what are you doing with the rest of your day?"

He thought for a minute. "Well, after I leave here, I am hanging out with my mom for the rest of the day, and then just chilling for work tomorrow."

They were face to face by now, and she leaned forward and kissed him. It had been a long time since he had been kissed, so he started out slowly, but after a few minutes his tongue was deep inside her mouth, and they were pulling off their clothes. He beheld her body, and she had some thickness to her form that was just right. She wrapped her legs around his waist and started moaning.

As G went to work, he whispered in her ear, "Breathe deep and let it go" as he rode her hard, like a jack hammer.

She asked him, "Is it good?"

He said, "The best," and they both started laughing.

G looked her in the face and said, "No questions until we're finished. I will then be able to tell you how good it was." As he hugged her and kept plunging the plunger inside, he felt her body tense up. As her nails clawed him in the back, he knew the doctor had made the patient well.

After about an hour and a half of different positions on the couch, on the floor, and eventually back in her bed, it was done. He took a quick shower, thanked her, and kissed her again as he left out the door. She was feeling good. G was good lover and not a one-minute man, and she thought, "Damn that was good." The rest of her day would be okay.

G drove back home thinking that he would not have a problem getting into the back room of the store from this point forward. He decided Lakeesha would not be told about this in any way, that there was just not a good way to say he had made love to another woman for his country.

When he got to the house, his mom was still at church, so he vacuumed the living room and the extra bedroom. He did not know if his mom would let Lakeesha sleep in his room. He would have to feel that out. He turned on the TV and watched an old western, bad guys in black hats terrorizing the town until a young guy comes to town and kills the bad guys. If he had to use the gun he had been issued, he would. He knew letting them kill a lot of people here was just not acceptable.

His mom came home and was in a good mood. She kissed him on the cheek and asked if he got the stuff from Lowes. He told her, "Yeah, I got everything, and I put the new filter in the furnace, vacuumed, washed the dishes, and mopped the kitchen."

She said, "Good. I will clean the bathroom and will put the nice linen on the bed in the extra bedroom. Are you hungry?"

He said, "No, I went to the Golden Corral while I was in Glen Burnie."

She said, "Okay. I will get some KFC because I don't feel like cooking, and by the time she gets here, she will probably have already eaten."

G nodded his head. "Sounds good, Ma. I can't wait for her to get here."

CHAPTER THIRTY-SEVEN

*R*ight about that time Mustapha gave Achmed a call. "What's up, brother?"

Achmed said, "Nothing. I'm just here lifting some barbells and watching some old football game that's on."

"Let's go shoot some hoops over at the park. I'll pick you up in ten minutes."

Achmed said, "Cool," and went and put on some shorts and his gym shoes. In a few minutes Mustapha pulled up, and Achmed jumped in the Escalade. They drove over to the park, on Washington Boulevard near Monroe Street. There were about thirty guys shooting hoops on the four rims.

Achmed walked up and asked, "Who's got next?" Three guys lifted their hands. "So you need two more?"

One of the guys said, "Yeah, you're okay. You two can run with us. Some of these guys only like to play with their own little squad."

Achmed and Mustapha started stretching and were watching the guys working together setting screens and passing to the open man. There was a lot smack talking going on.

"You can't check me!" said one of the ballers to the another as he blew by the guy for a layup.

When the game was over, and Achmed and Mustapha's team was up. They could tell that the other team was used to playing with each other. Achmed quickly identified the best player on the other team and told one of his teammates, "Let's switch. Let me check him."

The other guy heard the challenge in Achmed's voice. The guy with the ball tried to quickly go around Achmed with the ball, but he did not know that Achmed was a baller, too. Achmed tapped the ball away from the guy, and Achmed's teammate grabbed it and threw a quick pass to Achmed who was running the break and slammed the ball through the hoop.

Everybody around the court said, "Wow, we have a game!"

Both teams played hard, and it was a struggle. Achmed's team won by one off a nice pass from Mustapha. When it was over Achmed and Mustapha told the guys they were worn out and somebody else could get their spot.

The guys gave them five and said, "Come back and play with us again anytime! That was a good game."

Mustapha had some bottled water in the back of his Escalade, and he grabbed them a couple of bottles. Each bottle had a picture of a palm tree on it.

Achmed asked, "What's this?"

Mustapha said, "It's Caribbean bottled water, good stuff. We're going to start carrying it at the grocery store next week."

As he turned the bottle up and drank three large swallows, Achmed did the same and said, "Damn, that is good."

Mustapha said, "You seem ready for tomorrow. Get a good night sleep. I will pick you up first thing in the morning about 8:00am."

Achmed said, "I'm good. When I get home, I'll take a shower, watch a little TV, and turn in early."

Mustapha said, "Sounds like a plan."

They got into the Escalade and rode back over to the hood. After Mustapha dropped him off, he dialed Anthony's cell phone number and left a message that everything was good.

Anthony was downstairs in another hotel room talking with one of his other buddies from the brotherhood, Nate Washington, whom Mustapaha and Achmed had never met. They were discussing the gun that would be used tomorrow. Nate explained that it been bought off the streets and that it had no serial numbers on it. He recommended that the shooter put it in a plastic bag and a brown paper bag and throw it in the Anacostia River as they drove back from DC.

Anthony listened very intently. This brother had already thought about disposal of the weapon. He would provide them with a van that would be parked in the Lexington Market parking lot. Inside would be a delivery service logo that could be slapped on its side once they neared the home of the Hindu.

Anthony asked, "What is the tag number?"

Nate replied, "734" as he handed him the key.

Anthony said, "It won't be a problem parking the Escalade there, will it?"

He said, "No, just pay for parking. You can park a car there for weeks. Just pay, and no questions are asked."

When they were done talking, they stood up and looked out the window over at the fort. "So how about the back up plan?"

"Other than the fort, everything is going according to plan. Materials are being acquired slowly without drawing any attention, and of course the target isn't going anywhere–it's been there for fifty years."

Anthony smiled and said, "Thanks, my brother. I will let the others know you have everything under control."

They shook hands and hugged, and Anthony left. When he got back to his room, he saw the cell phone on the dresser was blinking with voicemail. He checked the voicemail, and it was Mustapha saying everything was okay and that Achmed was fine and ready to go tomorrow.

Anthony looked at the photo that Nate had given him of Ghaji Panday, the Trinidadian Ambassador to the U.S. He looked about fifty years old on the picture, Which had been taken as he entered the embassy. Anthony began fuming with anger as he looked at him. He knew he was directly involved with the death of his brother. He laid the picture down on the nightstand beside the bed and decided to watch a little TV. Tomorrow would be a busy day.

CHAPTER THIRTY-EIGHT

About 5:00pm G headed to the airport to pick up Lakeessha. He noticed that traffic was a bit light and was thankful that the airport parking lot was half empty so he could park up close. He got out of the car and did not see anyone just hanging around, so he walked across the street to the terminal to find her flight gate–29C, concourse C is where she would be coming out. Right about then a guy walked up to him and asked if he needed any help.

G just looked at him because the guy did not have on any airline jacket or anything, so G said, "No I don't need any help. Why do you ask?"

The guy said, "Because you look like you might be lost."

G looked around and said, "This is the airport, isn't it?"

The guy said, "Yes it is."

"Then I'm in the right place." G knew then the guy must be undercover security for the airport, so he would let him off the hook. G looked at him right in the eye and said, "I am a soldier stationed at Fort Meade, here to pick up a relative" and smiled at the guy.

The guy smiled back at him and said, "That's good. You have a military look about you, the right age and build. You know what I mean."

G said, "Yeah, I know what you mean. We're on the same team." The guy then did an about face and walked away. G felt good he said to himself, "The colonel has the airports covered, and probably the train stations, too. Good stuff."

Lakeesha walked out of her gate at 6:00pm on the dot. As she approached him, she started smiling. He opened his arms, gave her a big hug, and kissed her first on the cheek and then a good kiss on the lips. He felt her tongue slip into his mouth, and a real kiss started going there for a minute.

He said, "I'm so glad you came!"

She said, "I am glad I came, too. It is so good to see you. I wondered if we were ever going to see each other again, and lo and behold–here we are."

They walked down the stairs to the luggage area and waited on her bags. G asked how many, and she said only three, a suitcase and two smaller bags.

G just laughed and said, "That's good. I thought it might be three suitcases."

Once the bags came out they grabbed them and headed to the parking lot. He told her about the Altima he had bought upon getting back from Germany and when she saw it, she told him it was a nice looking car and that it fit him. "I'm sure all your friends must like it."

He thought to himself before answering, "Well, I don't have lots of friends; they did not have time for me before I got a car, so I don't have time for them now. Also, I have been really busy with work, and that's why I invited you here to meet my family and to see how I'm living, because really it's you that I care about. You know what I mean."

She looked at him and said, "I think so. I was just playing."

He said, "Yeah, I know. I just want you to know it's you that I like." As he drove her back to the house, he talked about the city and his plan to show her around after work tomorrow. She was all ears listening and looking at the city skyline as they drove up 295 to the city.

She said, "You have a big downtown. It looks bigger than Tampa's. Our downtown is not as high."

G told her that Baltimore always tries to compete with New York City. "A lot of New Yorkers moved here back in the fifties and tried to make Baltimore into a little New York."

She understood the comparison. The buildings did look like the buildings of New York she had seen on TV.

When they got to the house, Althea said, "Hello!" and gave Lakeesha a big hug. "How are you, Lakeesha? G has talked about you since the day he got back from Germany. I am glad you came, even though it's not the best of circumstances."

Lakeesha said, "I am sorry for your loss; I know it must be difficult."

Althea said, "We are trying hard to just remember her when she was vibrant and so alive. She was a God-loving person and never hurt anyone. Let me get your bag and show you the room."

They went upstairs, and G went and sat in the living room on the couch. After a few minutes they came back downstairs.

Althea said "We have some Kentucky Fried Chicken if you want, mashed potatoes and corn on the cob."

Lakeesha looked at G. "Have you eaten yet?"

G said, "No, I was waiting on you to get here before I ate."

So she said, "Sure, I will have a little bit of all of that."

Althea said, "Follow me into the kitchen; you are at home." They went into the kitchen to fix some plates.

G felt good; it seemed like his mom really did like her, and that was a good sign. He thought about Lisa for just a minute and then pushed the thought out of his mind. "That is work, this is true love."

When they came back into the living room, Lakeesha handed him a plate, and they all ate and watched TV together. Lakeesha and Althea talked about the women on television, how they were dressed and how they gave women a bad name being gold diggers. After a couple of hours, Althea said she was going to bed and would see them tomorrow. She had a busy day at work and was still handling family stuff for the funeral.

G moved over closer to Lakeesha on the couch and she laid her head on his chest and told him, "I can feel your heart beat."

He felt the warmth of her breast on his chest and she laid on him, wrapping her arms around him. She said, "You have gotten bigger since the last time I saw you. Are you working out?"

G smiled and said, "I'm doing my pushups and sit ups on a regular basis."

She said, "I can tell." She moved her hand down his pants and felt his manhood, she said, "And what about him? Have you been working him out as well?"

G was all smiles and said, "No, he's been waiting on you." He started kissing her. They laid on the couch and kissed for about thirty minutes when G said, "We probably should go upstairs. As he held her hand and walked her upstairs to the room his mom had prepared for Lakeesha, he held her tight and whispered in her ear and said, "Tomorrow night. I don't want my mom to say anything. She will be going over to my aunt's house tomorrow night, and then we can get loud."

Lakeesha started laughing. "That's okay. I don't want her to hear you screaming in ecstasy."

G just shook his head from side to side. "We will see who's screaming tomorrow, okay? Good night. I will wake you in the morning before I leave." They both went to bed with smiles on their faces.

CHAPTER THIRTY-NINE

Achmed awoke early about 05:30am and jumped in the shower, did some exercise, and then put on his clothes. He said a little prayer for strength and courage, ate a bowl of cereal, and waited for Mustapha to come and pick him up.

Mustapha woke up about the same time, turned on the TV to see what the weather was going to be like. "Sunny and about 70 degrees," said the weather woman. Mustapha could not help but notice she had a nice shape.

He decided to give Achmed a call. "Hey man, you woke?"

"Yeah," said Achmed.

"Cool. I'll be there in about twenty minutes."

Anthony was up in his room shaving and listening to the radio. The Isley brothers were on, an oldie but goodie said the DJ. "Fight it, fight the power!" Anthony was moving to the song almost like he was in a trance. He hated the system so much he could not wait to see the Hindu dead today.

Mustapha pulled up in front of Achmed's house, blew the horn, and Achmed walked out, looking up and down the street. He did not see anything out of the ordinary as he walked toward the Escalade and jumped in.

Mustapha smiled. "You ready, brother?"

Achmed said, "Yeah, let's do this."

As they drove over to the hotel to pick up Anthony, Mustapha flipped open his cell phone and speed-dialed him. Anthony picked up on the second ring. "Yeah, we'll be there in ten minutes."

Anthony said, "Good. I'll be in the lobby."

He grabbed the envelope from behind the drawer in the dresser where he always hid stuff. When staying in a hotel room, you never know who might come in, so for security purposes he always did this. He had put it there to hide it from anyone who may have come in his room even when he was asleep. He put on his clothes and went down to the lobby carrying his backpack and the envelope. Mustapha showed up and Achmed got out and jumped in the back seat. Anthony got in the front.

Mustapha said, "Good morning." Achmed did the same.

Anthony said, "Good morning, brothers. It is time. Let's go over to the Lexington Market parking lot." He started to explain what they would do. "First we go to the market parking lot. There will be a van parked there with the weapon inside in a floor compartment. We will then go to a cleaners and pick up two deliveryman uniforms, one of which is Achmed's size. We will then drive down Route 1 south to DC, avoiding the highway. We will go through as my friend told me last night the heart of chocolate city to southeast DC to a mechanics shop where you will get out of the van for a few hours and watch a little TV while I have a meeting with some of our DC brothers who will verify that the Hindu came to work today. About 4:30 we will go to his front door and Achmed will finish him off."

Achmed's heart was pumping as Anthony laid it all out. When they got to the parking lot, they saw the van and parked up on third level. They pulled beside it, and Anthony handed Mustapha a set of keys. They got in the van, and everything was just as Anthony had said. Up under the floor rug was a little compartment. Achmed opened it, and there was a 9mm Taurus handgun. Achmed released the clip. It had twelve rounds in it, and the serial number had been scraped off.

Anthony smiled and said, "Will that work for you?"

"Oh yeah, this will work."

They pulled out of the parking lot, and Mustapha asked, "Where is the this cleaners we're going to?"

Anthony said, "Green Mount and 31st Street on the east side."

Mustapha nodded his head, "I know where that's at."

As they drove over there, Anthony said, "From this point on, if we get stopped, we're delivery guys headed to DC where the office is in Anacostia. Drive the speed limit, use your blinkers, give the police no reason to stop us."

Mustapha nodded his head. He understood exactly what Anthony was saying. When they got to the cleaners, Anthony got out and went inside. It was a middle eastern-looking guy behind the counter. He handed him the ticket, and the guy punched in the numbers and the clothes started moving. He picked up two blue delivery uniforms and handed them to Anthony. Anthony said thanks and walked out on to Green Mount Avenue.

It was early in the morning, but there were a lot of people out catching buses and going into the check cashing palace and the chicken joint on the corner. Chicken sandwich for breakfast must be popular. Anthony laughed as he got back into the Escalade.

Mustapha asked, "What's funny?"

Anthony said, "Our people love chicken any time of day! I see the chicken joint is crowded early in the morning."

Achmed said, "If not a chicken sandwich they're getting a breakfast burrito. We like Mexican food, too!" and they all started laughing.

Mustapha guided the van down Route 1 to DC, and they all saw the difference once they hit the city limits. It truly was the chocolate city, and the women going to work and in and out of the office buildings were simply astounding.

Anthony said, "We need to recruit some of these sisters one day; they could have some value."

When they pulled into the mechanic shop, Achmed saw all the old beat up cars, and about fifteen black guys with some with oil and dirt on their hands wearing work clothes. Only two or three had on some casual clothes. He thought to himself, "These must be the DC brothers who are working the DC side of the house."

Anthony got out went over and spoke to them. They all looked over to Achmed and Mustapha and nodded their heads, but they did not come over and introduce themselves. Achmed thought to himself that that was ok, no names, just faces.

Anthony walked back to them and said, Someone is following the Hindu to work as we stand here right now, so everything is a go. Let me show you the TV room."

They walked inside the building. The place had a working air conditioner, a couple of couches, a television, a telephone, and some Black tail magazines on the table. Achmed opened up the magazine and a fine young lady was laying on her back, butt naked. "Yep, that's some Black tail all right," he mused as he turned on the TV. An old movie was on. He started to watch it, and the time seemed to fly by.

Right at 4:00pm Anthony walked in and said, "Let's go. I just got the call. He has left the office and is headed home. Achmed, here is the uniform. Put it on."

He slipped on the uniform and put his clothes in the bag that Anthony gave him. He gave him a fake beard and some sunglasses to wear as well. Anthony looked at Mustapha and asked, "You ready?"

Mustapha said, "Yeah."

They got into the van and drove up 10th Street and then over to Wisconsin, retracing the route they had taken before. When they got to the corner of the street, they saw the BMW in the driveway. Anthony looked back at Achmed as he slid the clip into the gun and pulled the slide back, putting a bullet in the chamber.

Anthony said, "Good luck" as he handed him a small brown bag that was supposed to be the package and a clipboard with a receipt attached.

They pulled up in front of the house, Achmed got out and walked to the door and rang the doorbell. A young girl about 11 or 12 answered the door.

Achmed smiled at her and said, "I have a package for Mr. Ghajji Panday. Is he home?"

She turned her head and yelled, "Daddy, it's for you!" and walked away.

In a moment he appeared walking down the hallway toward Achmed. Achmed smiled. As the man was about a foot away he asked, "You have a package for me?"

Achmed pulled the gun out from his pocket and in one smooth motion said, "This is from the brothers!" He fired pow, pow! One in the forehead and one in the chest. He was dead by the time his body hit the floor.

Achmed walked swiftly back to the van. He jumped in, and they sped away. The young girl and her mother rushed to the hallway to see their father/husband with blood pouring from his head and his chest. He was gone, and they both started screaming and crying.

Anthony patted Achmed on the shoulder from behind. "Is he dead?"

Achmed turned his head around so Anthony could see his face. "He is dead, and I told him this is from the brothers."

Achmed was grinning, and Mustapha was concentrating on getting back down to southeast with no cops.

Anthony said, "Give me the gun."

As Achmed handed it to him, Anthony put it in a plastic bag and then into a brown paper bag. When they got to the top of the Anacostia Bridge, Anthony looked around. There was no car immediately behind them, so he opened the window and threw the bag out into the Anacostia River.

When they got back to the mechanic shop, Anthony told Achmed to take off the uniform and to put his clothes back on. After that was done, they took the delivery sign off the side of the vehicle, and Anthony handed the keys to one of greasy guys who handed him the keys to an old blue Mazda Protégé.

Anthony smiled as he handed the keys to Mustapha and said, "This is our ride back to the Lexington Market parking lot."

Both Achmed and Mustapha were smiling now. Anthony asked what the big smiles were for, and Achmed said, "This is a plan in action, and just knowing that we are not driving back in the van, I feel good."

All of the other guys that they had seen earlier walked by and took a moment to shake their hands and pat them on the back, never saying a word. Achmed knew now he was truly a brother and would never have to take a back seat to anyone.

CHAPTER FORTY

*G*woke up that morning at about 6:00am, rolled out of bed, did about thirty push ups and thirty sit-ups, took a quick shower, put on clothes, walked down the hall, and peeked in on Lakeesha. She was still sleeping, so he walked over to the bed and sat down looking at her face. His soul was happy; his girl was here in his house with him. She was even more beautiful than she had been when they were in Bosnia. Her face was more womanly; she had put on a few more pounds all in the right places. He kissed her on the lips and said, "Good morning."

Her eyes opened and a big smile was on her face. "Good morning to you."

He told her, "I have to go to work, but my mom said she was going to take the day off and show you around downtown, okay?"

She said that was fine, so he kissed her again and was out the door. He turned on the radio when he got into the car, and there was nothing on the news station. When he got to the office

Randall was already there and was looking at the computer and asked him, "What's up?"

G said, "My girl got here last night, and man she is looking better than when I last saw her back in Bosnia. Fine, just straight up fine."

Randall started laughing. "See, I told you she's wife material. You better put a ring on her finger while she's here to let her know you're serious."

Right then one of the analysts walked up and said he had something to show them. When they got over to the board, they saw on the map that there had been a flurry of phone calls from disposable cell phones to some key numbers in Trinidad and Guyana in the Washington D.C. area. G had no idea what that meant, so he asked the analyst, "What's going on in Trinidad and Guyana that we need to know?"

The analyst explained, "A lot of people from India live in the Caribbean. Some of them are Hindu and some of them are Muslim. A few years ago there had been an attempted coup d'etat by Black Muslims in Trinidad who had a connection with Libya. It's all one big spider web. In Guyana you have the same dynamics, and of course a lot of them have immigrated to DC."

It started to make sense. G asked what were they saying.

"They mentioned that it was near cropover time, and that that the crop would be cut soon and then the party would start."

Randall said, "It's code for something, but what?"

G thanked the analyst and said, "Keep us informed if any of those calls start mentioning cannons, Star Spangled Banner, or Baltimore."

The analyst said, "No problem. I'm on it."

Randall asked G if he had breakfast yet.

G said, "No. I came straight over."

Randall said, "Let's get out of here and go down to the market and get a two dollar special." They decided to walk over to the Lexington Market. The market was open and doing big business selling breakfast. They ordered the sausage egg and cheese sandwiches and a cup of coffee for $2.50.

As G was eating, Randall said, "Something is about to go down. I wonder should we just recommend that they bust the guys we saw at the fort and just hold them?"

G thought about that and said, "We don't have enough to really hold them for long. We need more evidence so we can lock them up forever. I am going by Achmed's shop about 1:30pm this afternoon to see if I can get in the back room and see what's back there."

Randall said, "Cool. While you're doing that, I'll go over to the other market and see Lisa and watch the store and see if our old soldier has anything new to tell us."

When they finished their sandwiches, they walked out passed the parking lot and back to the office. They had missed seeing the Escalade enter the parking lot by only a few minutes. They went back to the office, and everybody was in the ops cell looking at the big screen TV. A bomb had just exploded on a cruise ship in Miami as it was pulling out to go on a cruise. So far twenty known dead and many more injured.

G looked at Randall and said, "What the hell is going on?"

Randall said, "We guessed a cruise ship here, but it's a cruise ship in Miami. I think we have to rethink everything now. Cruise ship security is about to tighten up, so is it realistic that they would hit a cruise ship here? We need to talk to the colonel."

G called over the analyst they had spoken with that morning and asked him how many analysts were working with him. He said about four.

G said, "I would like to meet with them in thirty minutes to go over everything we know or think we know about this cell operating in Baltimore." G looked at Randall. "Before we talk to the colonel, I would like to know what's in the back room of the store. We need some more clues. This is not as easy some might think. There are a whole lot of pieces to this puzzle."

Randall agreed and said, "Let's figure it out."

In thirty minutes they were all in the conference room, and G asked the analyst if they would put on the board what they knew, what they did not know, and what they thought was actually happening. They listed known phone calls to locations in Lebanon, Pakistan, Trinidad, and Guyana that were identified extremist on the other end, using coded conversations, with Baltimore being mentioned, cannons, and Fort McHenry. They had a clothing store guy along with three other suspicious guys at Fort McHenry looking like they were casing it for something, some type of attack against a ship going out or coming into the harbor, and an attack in Detroit and now Miami.

One of the analysts raised his hand. G said, "Speak up."

"Both Detroit and Miami have water by them, and it is believed the guys in Detroit fled across the river to Canada. I bet the guys who did Miami have already fled across the water to a nearby island."

G wrote that down as something to tell the colonel. G asked Randall, "Do you have any questions for these guys or thoughts you think they should consider?"

Randall said, "To me in my mind, I want to know what type of explosives did they use on the ship and how much is suspected was used. Do we have a notice out to hardware stores or farm equipment stores to keep up with whose buying stuff, and how much?"

The analyst wrote that down and said they would follow up.

G looked at them and said, "This is what I think. I'm thinking now Fort McHenry is a front for something else. It could be a target itself or it is to be used to target something more important, but our guys were not in Detroit or Miami, so this is much bigger than four guys. This is a coordinated set of attacks to instill fear and to paralyze people to scare them from living their everyday lives. We can't get into the group because they have known each other all their lives, and getting in that way is not going to work.

We have to use good detective techniques, find out whose buying explosive ingredients at those farm stores or hardware stores in small quantities but consistently coming back to get it. Check with the charter boat guys and ask of they have seen many foreigners or brothers from the hood, not your usual fishing brothers…" As he looked at everybody, he laughed. "Yeah, I know, but there are some brothers who truly like to fish."

The analysts started laughing too. They understood G was a city boy to his heart, but he was running this case and getting them involved and they liked that. "I've seen them fishing off the Hanover Street bridge all my life, and I have never ever seen them in a boat," he stated with his voice rising like a Baptist preacher.

As he started laughing, Randall said, "I believe you. Your city boys don't tend to go out on the big pond until they join the Navy. Us country boys, it's a different story," and the whole room chuckled. "Find out who has been chartering boats for the Chesapeake Bay, and what areas they have been wanting to go fish in the bay."

As G stood up and left the room, Randall thought, "This brother has leadership ability, and one day might be an officer if he decides to stay in."

When they got back to their cubicles, G asked Randall what he thought. Randall said, "You handled that meeting just as good as any Warrant Officer or Captain would have. You are a detective, so keep pushing us until we solve this case."

G said, "Fine." It was about 12:30pm, so he told Randall, "I'll make my way over to the shop. Do your thang over at the grocery store." Then G picked up the phone and called Lisa. "What's up?"

She said, "Nothing. Things are kind of slow, your typical Monday."

G said, "Cool. I'm headed over that way. Do you want anything to eat?"

She said, "Sure. You can get me some wings and French fries from the chicken shop down the street from here, and I'll pay you for it."

G started laughing. "Sure you will. I got you, don't worry about it. It's on me." G picked up a couple of chicken boxes with fries and some half and halfs, which is half lemonade and half Sprite, a Baltimore favorite. She was all smiles when he walked through the door. "Hello, my dear. How are you doing?"

She said, "Fine. You can set that over here" as she cleared off the counter she was standing behind and pulled up a chair so G could sit. She asked him how the rest of his day had been yesterday, and he told her it was okay. He and his mom had done a few things around the house, and his mom was handling parts of the funeral arrangements for his grandmother's funeral this upcoming Friday.

She said, "I'm sorry for your loss. I lost my grandmother a few years ago, not a good feeling."

G asked her where everybody was, and she said Achmed had called her at home yesterday and told her he would not be in today because he had to make a run out of town.

G's ears went up without him even noticing it. "And the other brother that works here?"

She said, "He's down the street getting something to eat. He should be back in a little while."

"That's cool. You basically are running this business. I'll have to figure out how to help you start your own," he said as he was eating a chicken wing.

She said, "Yeah, how you figuring that?"

G was eating and smiling all at the same time. "Let's just say I saved a little money while I was overseas and might be willing to become a partner in a business with you."

She continued eating her chicken, so he asked her what was her business going to be. She told him she had thought about what he said the other day about people taking cruises and bringing back the sodas and waters from the Caribbean. She has noticed that there is not a Caribbean store down here anywhere, but there are plenty of Caribbean people. "There is a vacant store over on Eutaw Street right across from Lexington Market that would be an ideal location. Way more people shop over there than they do on this side of Martin Luther King Boulevard."

G nodded his head as he was listening intently to her words and said, "I'm convinced." As he ate the last French fry, he motioned toward her and said, "I have something to give you," and leaned his head toward the back room.

She picked up on his motion and said, "Wait, let me put the 'Out to Lunch' sign up." She walked over to the window and placed the sign on the door and turned the lock. She led him to the back room, and he saw Achmed's office with the computer, the little safe chained to the floor with a very thick chain, and the couch and small bed over in the corner. They sat down on the couch.

He looked her in the eye and started whispering in her ear, "I am going to be your partner, if you will be my partner. No drama, just true friendship." He reached into his pocket and pulled out fifty $100 bills. "This is the start get the business license first; it don't cost much. Then check on the rent for the store. We can find suppliers for Caribbean stuff in New York City. Everybody I have ever met from the Caribbean says New York City and Miami are the hubs for anything you want. You feel me?"

She put her arms around his neck and said, "I feel you, G. You are a real brother."

He put his hand on her behind and pulled her close and said, "Even if the business takes time, remember to not quit because I believe in you." He laid her down on the small bed and kissed her for about thirty minutes. After that he asked her where was the bathroom, and she pointed down the hall. He went in to it and checked the cabinets for any drugs, looking under the sink for any strange looking chemical bottles. He did not see any, as he came back into the room she was not there. He thought immediately she must have gone back to the front to open the door. He went through the desk drawer and saw a few slips of paper with New York City on them like receipts from clothing suppliers. He quickly wrote down those addresses, and he noticed a flier for free shooting at Target One gun store in Severn. He wrote that down, too.

He closed the drawer and walked to the front. As she was moving quickly putting the chairs back up, she smiled at him and said, "G, you have made my day."

G said, "Lisa I was put here for a reason. I want you to be happy and to see your dream of having your own business come true. I've got to get back out there and sign up some more brothers and change some lives for the better. Give me a call later on and let me know where you're at." He kissed her on the lips and walked out the door.

Randall pulled into the Avenue Market parking lot and saw the old man standing by the door. The old man spoke first. "How's it going, Sarge?"

Randall said, "Fine, and how's it going with you?"

The old man whispered, "It's been pretty quiet around here the last few days. I have not seen the guys in the Escalade at all. They must be on vacation or working somewhere else."

Randall said, "That's good info," and slipped him a hundred dollar bill. "Keep on the lookout, and when you do see them here again give us a call. You do still have our telephone number, right?"

The old man nodded his head. "Yeah, I still have it. I have your card in my wallet."

After that Randall shook his hand and walked inside. He saw Keon up on the stand selling fruit drinks and he smiled and waved at her. She waved back. It had been a few days since he had last spoken to her, so he wondered if they were still good.

She came right down and hugged him and gave him a kiss on the lips. "Good to see you, stranger."

He laughed. "I have not been a stranger. I have just been busy with work. I apologize for not calling."

She said, "I understand; you're a busy man. When are we going to see each other again?"

"You're seeing me now," he said, "and later on tonight if you want."

She said, "That sounds good. About 7:00pm, my place? I'm cooking meat loaf tonight. Is that okay with you?"

"Sure, it's fine," he said. He told her he was going to walk around the market for a few minutes to see if he could spot any future recruits. "I'll be back in fifteen minutes."

She said, "All right, just don't recruit no females."

He looked at her and smiled, "You know you the only woman for me," and they both started laughing. So he walked around the market looking for anything strange or out of place near the grocery store. He did not see anyone who looked out of place or suspicious in any way, so he went back over to the fruit stand. He told Keon, "I will be on time for 7:00pm meatloaf and a movie."

She said, "It's only a movie."

He grinned. "And maybe an appetizer after the movie?"

She said, "That sounds better" and gave him a hug and he left.

When he got to his car, he turned on the radio. It was talking about the bombing in Miami and that security for the cruise ships out of Baltimore would be tightened. He was like, "Damn that was fast. They had to know that would happen, so why do it? Unless they're just faking us out. What else is in Baltimore worth attacking?" He decided he would go on the Internet and do a search of the most important things Baltimore was known for. Maybe he would notice something from the old reports that matched the Internet stuff.

When he pulled up, he saw G pulling in at the same time. "That's what I call clockwork," Randall said.

G smiled. "That's because we know what we are doing. If you stay too long, people start to wonder if you have a real job or what." G told Randall about the back room and the safe and the gun store flyer. "I'm going to write all this up in a report. Maybe the analyst will be able to put these locations on the map. I'm interested in this gun store. Severn is right next to Fort Meade."

Randall said, "Really? What's a city boy doing way out there at a gun store? Make sure they find out if he bought a gun from there or if he's using the place for target practice."

"Good," said G. "I'll ask that those questions be answered by the analyst in the report through liaison with the Severn police department."

They walked into the building and Randall told G what he had heard on the radio about security being enhanced at the Port of Baltimore for the cruise ships. G nodded and said, "We expected that. They had to expect that too, so what are they going after then? It can't be a cruise ship."

When they got back into the office, Randall told G since he was not from Baltimore, he would do a search on the Internet of the most important things Baltimore was known for to see the city from the eyes of a foreigner.

G said, "That's a good idea. I know what I think, but I was raised here. We need to see it from the eyes of a foreigner; it might be something different."

G looked up the gun store on the Internet and saw that it did have an indoor shooting range. He noted that as something he would bring up with Lisa. He looked up the clothing stores in New York City and they just came up as distributors in the garment district of New York City. He only guessed that they were probably owned by foreigners. He would have the analyst request liaison with the NYPD if they had anything on those establishments.

Randall typed up Baltimore famous sites and about ten things popped up: Camden Yard baseball stadium, Fort McHenry, Edgar Allen Poe's house, John Hopkins University and Hospital, Hippodrome Theater, Wood Lawn headquarters for social security, the National Aquarium, the Baltimore World Trade Center, Pimlico Race Track for the horse race the Preakness, and Union Station, the train station that Lincoln changed trains at as he rode to DC in disguise because of an assassination plot to kill him in Baltimore. Randall thought the train thing sounded interesting; he would check it out to see if any important people still took the train from Baltimore to DC by going down there later on this afternoon. He felt like a foreigner might find that interesting if they could actually carry out a similar attack. He spun around in his chair and told G what he had found and that he would go down to the train station to see if any important people use the train from Baltimore to DC.

G said, "That's a good idea. I'm wondering why Achmed had to go out of town, and the old man said he had not seen the Escalade in a couple of days. They might be closer to carrying out their plan than we think. Hopefully this report will generate some answers." It was about 4:40pm, so he told Randall, "Good luck at the train station. I'll see you in the morning. I'm going to pick up my girl and show her around downtown. We will go by the aquarium and the trade center."

G left the office and jumped in his car. When he turned on the radio, there was nothing spectacular on, just your usual music, as he sped to his house. When he opened the door, he could smell the food. He walked into the kitchen, and his mom and Lakeesha were preparing leg of lamb, with mash potatoes, and peas. It smelled wonderful.

"So, how are my two favorite ladies doing?"

His mom said, "Fine. We had a good day. I showed her around downtown and the market where we got this lovely leg of lamb."

Lakeesha said, "I see why you talked about your city so much; your downtown is bustling with people and just humming with activity."

G asked, "Did you see the aquarium or the world trade center?"

His mom said, "We walked by there going to the galleria, but we did not go in."

G said, "I will have to take you there probably tomorrow. This food is smelling too good to go out of the house after we eat."

His mother started laughing, "Yeah, both of y'all won't be able to move after a good dinner like this."

They both looked at each other, and G said it for both of them with his eyes, "Oh yeah, I will be able to move something tonight."

G went into the living room and turned on the TV, and breaking news came on across the screen from the DC channel. That's the good thing about Baltimore and DC being so close–they get both cities' channels.

The news reporter was standing in front of a house and said, "Breaking news: The ambassador from Trinidad to the United States was slain in his doorway about thirty minutes ago. The initial report by police is that a man in a delivery uniform lured the ambassador to the door and proceeded to shoot and kill the ambassador. He leaves behind a wife and three children. Damien James, News 4 reporting."

G was stunned. He had just been told about chatter about Trinidad this morning "crop over" and "cutting the crop," and he now knew what that meant. He would be on it first thing in the morning. He thought, "I wonder what the description of the shooter will be."

Lakeesha walked into the room and told him, "The food will be ready in just a few minutes."

He put his arms around her waist and said, "The food appears to be ready right now," and started giggling.

She did the same and said, "Be patient," and went back into the kitchen.

Meanwhile the FBI in DC had called in several of its top agents, and they were discussing the details of the report the young girl had made of a Black man, about 6'2", with a mustache and beard, wearing dark sunglasses. The agents shook their heads. That fit about a million Black men living in DC. She did not remember anything about the delivery uniform other than it was blue, also the color of choice for delivery men in DC.

They asked the agent in charge, "Who hated this guy back home in Trinidad? Better to look there for who benefits from this man's murder then point the finger at a bunch of people here."

The lead FBI agent agreed, "This was not a robbery; this was a hit, pure and simple. Politics back in Trinidad. I'll let the big guys know we're working it, but we don't have any real clues. Maybe ballistics will be able to tell us about the weapon used. I noticed that there was no shell casings, so he picked them up too, a real pro. None of the neighbors saw anything; everybody was in their houses, and they all said the same thing…that he was a nice guy and appeared to be a family man. They knew he was a diplomat, but Trinidad would not have been a country that would have one of its diplomats assassinated, in their opinion. One of the neighbors said maybe he was having an affair with a DC woman. You know how these DC men are about their women."

The agent nodded his head and said, "We will check into that." He walked over to the other agents and told them what one of the neighbors had said about a woman and maybe a jealous boyfriend. He said, "Ask his staff if he has been seen with a woman other than his wife lately. You never know; the neighbor brought it up for a reason. Maybe he saw him with somebody."

They all agreed that in DC, it was possible.

CHAPTER FORTY-ONE

*W*hen Achmed was dropped off at his house, he went inside and jumped in the shower. He turned the water on hot and took a long time under the water. He had finally done what his father had told him must be done: For the enemy to take his hands off the righteous, blood would have to be spilt. He was tired of the bullshit in this world and would kill as many as it took to bring about change.

After showering he turned on the television, and it was on the news that the ambassador from Trinidad had been killed in his own doorway. Initial reports said there could have been a love interest involved, but that was off the record since the investigation was still ongoing. Achmed smiled. "They're on the wrong track already! Love interest. They keep on thinking that way, and we won't have to worry about them clowns." He fixed himself a bowl of cereal and watched a basketball game until he fell asleep.

Mustapha drove Anthony back to the parking lot and parked the Mazda beside the escalade. He handed the keys and the parking tickets to Anthony, and they drove back to Anthony's hotel. Along the way Anthony said, "Keep an eye on Achmed; make sure he is not affected by today's events–no boasting or bragging. You say the wrong thing around the wrong person, and it could be over just like that."

Mustapha said, "No problem. I will check on him tomorrow. What's next on our agenda?"

Anthony said, "We need to give Khalid some work. There is a power station in Baltimore that provides power for DC all the way up to Philadelphia. We need to turn out the lights. Give him a call and tell him to be ready on Wednesday."

Mustapha said, "Okay, sounds good. We're not taking a break."

"No way," said Anthony. "Keep them dazed and confused— that's the best way to go," as he got out of the car and headed to his room.

CHAPTER FORTY-TWO

*A*fter eating dinner, G gathered up everybody's plates and quickly washed them. His mom said she was going over to Melody's house to finish arrangements for the funeral; they were still writing the obituary. G said okay.

Lakeesha came into the kitchen with G and started drying the plates and putting them back into the cabinet. He told her how happy he was that she was there and gave her a big hug and kiss. She kissed him back with feeling. They were alone, and she wanted him, and he wanted her. He led her by the hand upstairs to his bedroom and turned on the radio. The music was soft as he started pulling her clothes off. He beheld her form and thought, "My, she is fine!"

She pulled off his shirt, felt his muscles, and said, "You are a beautiful man, G."

As usual, G had something funny to say. "Well, I have been working out a lot lately...."

Then they made love. When all the moaning and screaming was done, he held her in his arms and said, "I've got something to ask you."

She said, "Go ahead and ask."

"I was thinking, perhaps we should be a couple, and if you want to get married, I would like to marry you."

She looked at him. "Are you sure you want to get married, or do you want me to move here and be with you?"

He answered, "I want to marry you. I think we are good for each other. I don't want to interfere with your finishing college, though."

She said, "I can finish school here. Just promise me to stay the nice man that you are. You don't have to change and be somebody that you're not—I love you just as you are!"

With that, they kissed until they fell asleep. When the morning came, G was up early and in the shower, humming and singing.

Before he could turn around, Lakeesha had joined him in the shower. Things got hot and heavy. G was definitely not used to a woman giving of herself like this before. He almost did not want to go to work because he felt so good.

He hugged her and said, "Baby, I got to go to work. I'm coming straight home to you when I get off. You can tell your mom that we are getting married. I love you!"

He rushed out the door to the office, which was humming. The analyst walked up to him as soon as he sat down at his desk. "We've got some answers for you. There has been a report out by ATF that small portions of fertilizer have been bought by different people not enough to register, but the numbers for various stores in the Baltimore area are up. They believe someone is putting together a bomb, but they don't know who. The Trinidadian phone calls appear to have been code for the hit on the ambassador yesterday, so we know what cropover meant."

G nodded. "Any idea where these calls were made from–DC or Baltimore,?"

"Yes, southeast DC and Park Heights/Baltimore."

G told them, "There is a club in Park Heights called the Blue Caribbean, and that's where all the islanders in the city party. Most of them live in that area, so concentrate there. What about the description of the shooter?"

The analyst said, "Black male, about six feet tall, beard and mustache, blue uniform, wearing dark sunglasses."

G thought, "That could be our boy, Achmed. So, he might be a killer." G looked over at Randall's empty desk. He was not in yet. "He must have had a good time over at Keon's. Time to start packing; we might have to do some shooting ourselves here shortly."

Randall walked in looking tired. G asked, "What's up? Didn't get any sleep last night?"

Randall smiled, "Not really. I think I'm engaged."

G started laughing. "Well, you're not alone. I asked Lakeesha to marry me, and she said yes."

Randall said, "Keon asked me and let me know that she was not about to let a good man like me come and go in her life, so I told her let's see how being engaged works for a couple of months."

The analyst said, "And one last thing: Achmed Jackson, Mustapha Hampsho, Khalid Quasim, and Jahil Julani have used the target gun store range about five different times during the last twelve months, using their own weapons, 9mms."

G looked at Randall. "So, they have been practicing pulling the trigger. That makes it easy to pull it on a real person. I think they had something to do with the killing yesterday."

Randall had not heard. "What killing?"

"The ambassador from Trinidad was gunned down in his home doorway yesterday afternoon."

Randall's eyes got wide. "The phone calls and the killing are connected!"

G said, "Yeah, they're murderers. We need to keep our weapons close from now on."

Randall reached into the desk drawer and handed G his 9mm and said, "Keep it on you, especially when you go by the clothing store."

When Althea got up and took her shower, Lakeesha was downstairs already, fixing breakfast. She told her, "You did not have to cook!"

Lakeesha said it was no problem and that she had something to ask her.

Althea said, "Sure, what is it?" as they sat down at the kitchen table.

Lakeesha said, "G asked me to marry him last night, and I wanted to know what you think. Are we too young? Should we wait, or what?"

Althea smiled and said, "I think if you love him, you should marry him because you never know when he might leave here. Love is not something you can put on a time table. I know he loves you. When he talks about you, he has a glimmer in his eye that I have only seen on a few occasions in a man about a woman–my father about my mother, and my husband John when he would be talking about me to his brother. So, you take love while you can and give it all you got," and she gave her a big hug.

Lakeesha smiled and said, "I want to call my mom and tell her."

Althea said, "Go ahead; we won't leave to go downtown for a while. Let's let the stores open up."

Meanwhile, the colonel was down at the Pentagon at a meeting with the general and all the military city detachment commanders. The Miami commander was briefing everyone on the clues that they had and that they had missed as a cruise ship being the actual target. They had concentrated on the airport since so many flights came there from overseas, and they had focused on Miami Beach being a target since so many tourists came there. The information was that the explosion had happened on two decks where people were near the swimming pool and the casino. Either backpacks or small duffel bags were used and dynamite or C4 was the explosives; twenty-two were dead and about fifty injured. No one had called in responsibility for the attack. Several of the dead were actual boat workers, and their backgrounds were being checked out.

The general told everyone to follow up on every lead and to leave no stone unturned, "Spend some money. People will talk when money is being spent. Catch these guys before they kill again."

On the ride back to Baltimore, the colonel thought to himself, "These guys are planning to hit something we have not been watching." He would do a round table with the analyst when he got back to the office. When he stepped in the door, he told his secretary to call everybody into the briefing room.

G and Randall came in and took seats. All the analysts and other support people came in and sat along the wall. The colonel stood up and said, "The Miami attack was a surprise. All of our leads had pointed at the airport or Miami Beach as the target, and it ended up being a cruise ship. All of our leads have been to Fort McHenry. I think it is something else. Find out what else is important in this city. I have guys covering the airport and the train station. Find out what else they would consider an important punch. Agents, start spending some cash. The general has said spend money and people will talk. Go into stores and shops and ask people about anything out of the ordinary; then get back with me when you have something."

Randall and G walked back to their desks, and G asked Randall, "Did you see anything strange at the train station?"

Randall said, "No. I did ask the lady in the information desk if any important people take the train from here, and she said yes; most of the congressmen from the east coast take the train to DC. It's a smoother ride and much quicker than taking I-95. Did you notice any security there?"

Randall said, "Yeah, I saw a couple of uniformed Baltimore police officers. They looked like they were keeping the homeless from setting up in the station."

G said, "That's good, so the airport is covered, the train station is covered, and the cruise ships are now covered. What's not covered? Let's go look at the map of the city in the briefing room."

They both stared at the map. They saw the tunnel. "What about the tunnel? Is there any special security on the tunnel?" asked Randall.

"I don't know. We can request it by putting it in a report and recommend the tunnel be covered." They were getting frustrated, not knowing what was happening.

Randall said, "We need to follow the Escalade tomorrow and see where it goes."

G said, "That works for me. Bring a hat or some sunglasses so they can't see our faces, but we will follow them from the market. I'll see you at eight in the morning."

Randall asked, "And where are you going now?"

G looked at him and said, "I'm going to Jared and get my girl a ring."

Randall couldn't help it. He had to say something. "Oh, he's going to Jared!" and started laughing.

G said, "Forget you!" as he walked out of the room. G made his way to the mall and walked into the jewelry store. A young lady asked if she could help him.

He said, "Yes, I'm looking for an engagement ring for my girlfriend."

She said, "Congratulations. Do you know her ring size?"

Chapter Forty-two

G said, "No, I don't."

"Well, I don't recommend you buy a ring without knowing her ring size. You should both come in together so you know what you're getting–a ring that she likes and that fits."

G said, "That's a good idea. Thanks, I will be back, and I will make sure you get credit for the sale. What's your name?"

She said, "Pearl."

"Oh, that's a nice name. I don't think I have ever met a girl named Pearl."

"And you probably never will again," she smiled back.

G drove back home. Lakeesha and his mom were not back yet, so he turned on the TV news. It told the story about a young New Yorker who was visiting relatives in Baltimore and was found dead from a gunshot wound outside of the Eden Lounge. He had been a Marine who had served his country honorably and was visiting relatives. Just like that, his life was taken for no real reason. G thought, "Something has to be done. There is war overseas and a war going on right here. I have to keep the faith and stay strong."

Right about then the ladies walked into the house. G asked, "How was your day?"

They said fine; they had been shopping and bought a couple of dresses.

G said, "Mom, we're going to make a run to the jewelry store. We will be right back," as he grabbed Lakeesha's hand and walked out the door. He kissed her on the lips when they got into the car, "I went by the store earlier, and the saleslady said to make sure we got the right size, I should bring you there."

She smiled and said, "That's a good idea."

When they got there, Pearl was still there. G walked over to her and asked if she could help them with the ring.

She responded, "Sure I can," as she walked behind the counter where the engagement rings were.

Lakeesha saw one that she liked and said, "That one right there. I like that one." It was a beautiful ring, and G liked it too. It was a good sized rock that said "somebody loves you." He asked the lady how much.

She said, "It's three thousand."

Lakeesha smiled and said, "We'll take it. When will it be ready?"

Pearl said, "The ring fitter will measure your finger and size the ring so it won't be slipping off. It should be ready by tomorrow afternoon."

Lakeesha watched as G went into his pocket, pulled out a roll of hundred dollar bills, and counted out three thousand dollars. The lady gave him a receipt, and they headed back home.

She told him, "I like the way you handled that–no questions; you just paid for it."

He looked at her and said, "Because I love you and I want you to know that."

She held his hand as he drove back to the house. When they got there, his mom had made them some sandwiches and potato chips and some sodas. It was all good as they watched the Wheel of Fortune together and tried to guess the words. When it got late, they went to bed and since they were now engaged, they did not hide that they were sleeping together. G fell asleep with her in his arms and slept a deep sleep.

He awoke the next day feeling like a new man. He had a woman to take care of from this point forward. Handling Lisa would be difficult because he did not want to hurt her feelings, so he was going to have to convince her to help him, help herself, and help Baltimore all at the same time. He kissed Lakeesha on the cheek as he left to go to work.

When G got there, Randall was already there and had a new backpack full of cash. G asked him how much he had gotten, and he said the captain had given him fifty thousand dollars, and told him not to bring it back.

G smiled at that and said, "We have to use this the right way, and I guarantee you we will get some information."

Randall asked, "Where should we go first?"

G said, "I know it's early in the day, but this is probably the best time to go by the strippers club. Our boys may have been out celebrating lately with the ladies, and if they spent some money, the ladies will remember them."

They headed over to the El Dorado Club on Baltimore Street. When they walked in, it looked like it had been a good night. There were empty bottles stacked high in the trash can, and two middle age brothers were behind the bar. There were no ladies dancing, but the juke box was playing.

One of the bartenders asked, "What can I do for you two gentleman?"

G leaned on the bar and said, "It's kind of early, but I would like to see some booty. I just got engaged, and it might be awhile before I see some different ass, if you know what I mean." He slid a fifty dollar bill to the brother. "I'll have a cranberry juice with that, and you can keep the change."

The brother smiled and hit the buzzer under the bar. All of a sudden and out of nowhere three sisters appeared, and they were not bad looking. One got up on the stage and started dancing, and the other two came and sat beside Randall and G, making small talk. "So, what's happening, cutie? What brings you out so early in the morning?"

"Just hanging out," said G. The two guys behind the bar were whispering to each other since G had said keep the change. He told the young lady, "I'll be with you in a moment," and gestured for one of the guys to come over.

He walked over and said, "What's wrong? You don't like these?"

G said, "No, that's not the problem. I just have a few questions I wanted to ask you since you look like you run things around here."

The guy's eyebrows went up. He said, "Maybe, but I'm not the owner."

G said, "I'm in the army, me and my partner here. Did you hear about what happened in Miami the other day and Detroit a couple of weeks ago?"

The guy said, "Yes, I heard about that shit. What's up?"

"Well, we don't want that to happen here in Baltimore, and we heard a rumor that the guys involved here were throwing around some big money in the last couple of weeks and that they probably came here. I did not want to ask the ladies about them and get them all upset. I figured if you asked them, they might remember things better. It was four or five guys, a Black guy and some Arabs. Do they ring a bell?" He slid three one hundred dollar bills to the guy.

He thought about it and said, "When did you say they were here?"

"Within the last month for sure, driving a white Escalade."

The guy got a big smile on his face and said, "Yeah, I remember them; they were throwing a welcome party for one of them. I remember when they parked, he parked it taking up two spaces. The Arab did not want anybody scratching up his ride."

G looked at Randall, and Randall nodded his head as he handled both ladies. He had bought them both twelve dollar drinks, so they were happy, and he had slid a fifty into each of their garter belts, so they were very happy.

G asked the guy, "Can you ask the ladies if the guest of honor ever said where he was from?" as he slipped him another three hundred dollars. The brother snapped up the three bills quicker than a crab on a shrimp and motioned the ladies over to him. G watched as the guy handed the ladies one hundred dollars each. When he walked back over to G, he smiled and said, "Trinidad, the brother was from Trinidad, light-skinned complexion like Debarge, could pass for an Arab if you did not look close enough."

G said, "Thanks, brother, we were never here on this, but we will be back to give you some business."

The brother looked at them and said, "I hope you get them before they hurt anybody else; life is too short for all the dumb shit."

G said, "I agree, my brother. I'm about to get married, and all I want is to be with my girl and start a family, but I got to do this first."

The guy stretched out his hand and shook his and Randall's hands, and said, "America first, semper fi, former Marine, do your thing."

G walked out of the club and said to Randall, "We have our connection now. Trinidad hit was for this guy and Achmed did it, probably to prove something to this guy. Let's head over to the market; it should be open by now."

They drove over to the market. Randall was shaking his head. G asked him, "What's up?"

Randall said, "Both of them honeys were fine. I asked them what else do they do, and they said nothing, dancing pays better than any little job they could get, and they'd rather dance than work for little to nothing."

When they got over to the market, they saw the white Escalade was already there, so they slipped on their baseball caps and dark sunglasses. G did not see the old man, so he figured maybe he was taking the day off or something. He called the analyst on his cell phone and told him that the Trinidadian had been directly involved and to check the flights and names from the past two weeks since he probably arrived within the last month.

The analyst said, "I'm on it, sir. I'll have a list of names when you get back."

G said, "Roger out." G was taken a little aback that the analyst had called him sir, since he was only an NCO.

Randall asked, "Do you want me to go in?"

G said, "Let's wait and see if they come out. I would rather not be seen here in case we have to follow him in wherever he goes."

Randall said, "Good idea," and just about then out the door came Mustapha, and off he went heading downtown.

G followed from a good half a block away. He took Pennsylvania south to Pratt Street, made a left, and made a right on President's Street to Alcieana and pulled right in front of the Water Front Marriott Hotel.

G told Randall to get out and watch from the corner, and then he drove around the traffic circle a couple of times. In about a minute, Anthony walked out and got in the front seat of the Escalade. Randall recognized him from the fort and walked back over to the car and got in.

G said, "Did you get a good look at him?"

Randall said, "Yeah, it's the same guy that was with them at the fort."

G said, "Yeah, that's him, the Trinidadian."

Randall asked, "Are we going to follow them?"

"No, they might notice us. We need to let the colonel know. He knows some guys who can go into his room without him noticing it." They rushed back to the office.

CHAPTER FORTY-THREE

Mustapha asked Anthony, "Where to?" when he got in the car.

Anthony said, "Take me over to the warehouse your boy has set aside for our use. I want to see it to see if it is suitable for putting together our package."

Mustapha smiled and steered the car across town over into the Cherry Hill area where the abandoned warehouse was located. He had the key on his key ring. When they went inside, it was barren and had some old bench tables inside of it, but the electrical worked. Mustapha went in the back and flushed the toilets, and the water was working, Mustapha asked, "Will this work?"

Anthony said yes as he flipped open his cell phone and called Nate. "The box is open and ready to be filled" and gave him the address. Anthony then said to Mustapha, "Let's go; I'm hungry. Leave the door unlocked so they can come in and do what they have to do."

Achmed went in to work, and Lisa was upbeat and perky. "Good morning; how are you?" he asked. She said she was doing good. He asked, "What's up? Must be a boyfriend."

She smiled, "How could you guess?"

"Because you're so perky this morning. He must have hit that spot."

She just shook her head at him and said, "That's the first thing everybody thinks, that if you're hitting the spot you can do anything you want. A woman wants more."

Achmed said, "Yeah, yeah, I know" as he walked into the back room. He sat down at his desk, turned on the computer, and checked the news. He did not notice anything out of place on his desk or on the little bed. As he read the news, there was not anything new on the ambassador's killing. He checked several news sites on the story to include the Trinidadian newspapers. He opened up his safe grabbed his 9mm and put it in his waistband, counted up the money and said, "Business needs to pick up. I am going to have to make a run to New York City shortly." He was looking forward to looking all the old guys in the face now, and they would know he was a true believer.

He went out front. Lisa was folding up shirts and humming. He asked her who the new boyfriend was, was it anybody he knew, and she said, "No, he's a Dunbar boy from the other side of town."

That was all he needed to hear; he did not have a high regard for the Dunbar guys as they all thought they were going to the NBA, and only a couple would ever make it. He looked at her and said, "Good luck with that" with a little smirk on his face.

She said thanks, and in her mind she said, "You just don't know; G is a real brother and supporter of a sister and her dreams. All you do is love 'em and leave 'em, just like all the rest." So she smiled at him, but was not smiling with him.

Achmed stepped outside just to see what was happening on the street. It was a typical day already, with folks selling everything out on the street from flip flops to little TVs.

CHAPTER FORTY-FOUR

When G walked in, all the analysts walked up to him and patted him on the back for a job well done on locating the Trinidadian. They showed him a list of Trinidadians' names that flew into BWI in the last couple of weeks.

G said, "Crosscheck that list with names of men staying at the Waterfront Marriott, and we have identified our number one target. I need to speak with the colonel."

The analyst said, "We're on it."

G asked the colonel's secretary if he was in, and she said, "Yes, he's in the office."

"Could you let him know that Steen would like a minute of his time?"

She said sure and used the intercom to speak with the colonel. She said, "Go right in," and he and Randall went in. The colonel looked a bit tired, like he had been up all night, and swung his chair around to them.

"Sir, we have identified the Trinidadian. He is staying at the Waterfront Marriott Hotel; we saw him get picked up by the white Escalade this morning and have verified that they have been practicing shooting right outside Fort Meade and that they have purchased 9mms. Their whereabouts are unaccounted for on the day of the assassination of the ambassador. I think a room search is in order when he's out of the hotel room."

The colonel nodded. "I agree. I will have those Special Forces guys from Bragg handle that. Get me a room number, and we will have that set up by the end of the day. Any idea of what the real target is yet?"

"Not yet, sir, but I am sure they will lead us to it. We will follow them again tomorrow." Then he looked at both of them and said, "Be careful; they have already killed once, so killing the second time is real easy."

G and Randall stood up and saluted, and G said, "We'll be careful."

The colonel said, "I heard a rumor you're getting married" and smiled at him.

Randall shrugged as if to say, "It wasn't me who told him."

The colonel said, "I have my sources around here, too. Congratulations, Steen. Now get out of here and find that target." When they left the room, the colonel got on the phone and called Major Smith and told him the details and that he wanted that room searched by the next night.

Major Smith said, "Will do, sir; as soon as we get a room number, my guys are on it. We will get both rooms on either side to listen in on what is being said, and when we verify that Elvis has left the building, we're going in."

The colonel said, "Good. I can always depend on the SF guys to get the job done." He spun around in his chair and just stared at the map of Baltimore, wondering what their target really was.

Althea and Lakeesha were downtown window shopping and sightseeing with Althea acting as tour guide. They went by the aquarium and walked by the trade center up Light Street to the financial district where all the banks were located, and she pointed out the Federal Reserve Bank of Baltimore, a big building. Althea told her this was a special branch that handled all the foreign accounts from foreign banks. Althea had a girlfriend who worked there who told her it handled trillions of dollars in transactions every month.

CHAPTER FORTY-FIVE

Nate pulled up to the warehouse and started unloading bags of fertilizer and other white buckets of chemicals. Nate had studied chemistry in college and knew what he was doing, but Anthony was even better than he was, and he gave him the added knowledge to make the bomb more effective. The goal was to destroy the building completely. With all its records and equipment being no longer usable, the people would be hard to replace. With their inside knowledge of the operations of the bank, they were going to free the Third World from debt slavery. Since all the records would be destroyed, no one would know what was still owed. They had been assured that the back up tapes that were on another floor would be destroy as well. Fort McHenry would be used to attack a British ship on the same day at the same time, as well as city hall. The whole city would be paralyzed.

Mustapha and Anthony stopped at a little restaurant on Washington Boulevard run by some Jamaicans. Mustapha ordered up some jerk chicken and had a conversation with the barmaid. She told him that her family was from Jamaica, but she had been born here. He complimented her on her accent. She said she got it from her parents and asked him what brought him to Baltimore. He told her school, the University of Baltimore, that he was studying business. He ate his food and watched the big screen TV.

The news came on, announcing that there had been a break in the investigation of the killing of the Trinidadian ambassador. Information from Trinidad stated it was a political assassination and not a crime of passion as had originally been thought. Anthony and Mustapha looked at one another. Mustapha asked for the check while Anthony went into the bathroom to wash his hands, and looked into the mirror and thought to himself, what idiot talked. He then walked out of the restaurant. He was pissed about what had been might have been said back in Trinidad and wondered who, if anyone had given the plan away. He would have to push up his timetable.

Mustapha came out of the restaurant and said, "What do you think? Do they know you're here?"

Anthony smiled and said, "I doubt it, but we need top speed things up. Call Khalid and cancel tomorrow's train station appointment."

The FBI agent liaison representative in Trinidad had reported to headquarters that the word on the street in Port of Spain was that the Black Muslimen had taken their revenge on the ambassador. The FBI figured they would put the story out to rattle somebody's cage. An analyst told G about the breaking news that the FBI was reporting that the assassination was linked to the Black Muslims as a revenge attack and that it was on the news.

G said, "Oh, that's not good. Our boy may make a run for it. Call the colonel and tell him we need to put a tail on the

Escalade now. Our boy might check out of the hotel, and we'll never see him again."

Anthony called Nate and asked him how far he had gotten.

Nate said, "I'm almost done. I wanted you to see it to give it that final touch."

Anthony said, "We don't have time put it together. Meet me in front of the building in ten minutes."

Nate was excited as he twisted the wires together and put everything in the U-haul truck.

Anthony told Mustapha, "Take me back to the hotel. I'm checking out, and we go today. Call Achmed call him and tell him to meet us on Light Street in front of the Federal Building."

Mustapha made the call. Achmed said, "What's up?"

Mustapha said, "It's a go today. Meet us on Light Street in front of the Federal Building."

G and Randall jumped in the Altima and flew over to the hotel. As they were approaching, they saw Anthony with a suitcase and a duffel bag getting into the Escalade. G said, "He's leaving, man. That report has him spooked that he's been ratted out. Follow him."

As they wove through downtown, they stopped on Light Street and got out and started talking. G called in their location to the analyst and told him to let the colonel know that it looked like they were about to do something.

The colonel yelled out, "Shoot them now before something blows up."

G could hear the colonel's voice over his cell phone, and right at that moment he saw out of the corner of his eye his mom and Lakeesha walked past Anthony. His heart almost fell out of his chest. He saw Achmed pull up, and they all walked up to the U-haul. G looked at Randle and said, "We have to act now!"

They both ran as fast they could, pulling out their 9mms and started firing. Pow, pow, pow! Anthony took one in the chest. Mustapha took a couple in the side. Nate was running down the street, and Randall was running after him, firing. He hit him twice in the back, and he fell to the street.

Randall told him, "Don't move; you're under arrest." Achmed pulled out his 9mm and fired a couple of shots. Pow, pow! G ducked, covered, and rolled, and came up firing. He hit Achmed center mass in the chest.

G leaned over him and asked him, "Why, brother?"

Achmed said, "For my father." Achmed, coughing up blood, asked G, "Why, brother?"

And G said, "For my father, and my city Baltimore, do or die." He looked and saw that his mom and Lakeesha were okay. They were across the street, watching in amazement as G was in the middle of a gun fight. They thought he was a recruiter.

Someone in the crowd said, "Those two guys just stopped a terrorist attack!"

When the police arrived, Randall whipped out his permit and said, "U.S. Army."

The cops echoed, "U.S. Army?"

G said, "Yes, U.S. Army, defending the home front. Colonel Briley's guys. I'm sure he's on the way down here."

Within a few minutes Colonel Briley was on the scene, talking with the Baltimore Chief of Police and the FBI who showed up. The colonel came up to both of them and said, "Great job! You saved hundreds of lives today. Head back to the office and write up your reports."

They both said, "Yes, sir."

G walked across the street and hugged his mom and Lakeesha. "I guess you know I do more than help the recruiters now, eh?"

They both looked at him, and his mom said, "I'm so proud of you!"

Lakeesha hugged him and said, "I knew you were special from that first day I saw you," and she gave a him a kiss.

G and Randle went back to office, and when they walked in, all the analysts and support staff started clapping and cheering, "You got them, you got them!" As everyone was walking up and slapping them on the back and hugging them, the analyst said, "You two have made every analyst in here proud; you made this operation a success."

When they sat down and wrote their reports and checked the block for case closed, they felt real satisfaction.

The colonel came in and said, "I'm putting you both in for the Legion of Merit. The President will be made known of your efforts and contributions to the safety and security of this nation."

G told Randall, "I'm headed home, Randall."

"Cool. See you tomorrow."

G drove home slowly. His heart was still beating hard, and when he walked in the door, his whole family was in the house. All his cousins had heard the news about the gun battle on Light Street with terrorists, and the word had spread like wildfire on the block that G was in it and had killed several terrorists.

His cousin Rashim walked up to him and hugged him and said, "You are a soldier, and now I know you're the righteous brother around here. I understand why you joined the army now. They thought they could walk all over B'more. You showed them—you come here, you better act like you know somebody!"

Everybody in the room started laughing, and someone from across the room hollered, "RESPECT! G pushed back today. They know now don't bring that BS here, don't start none, won't be none."

His aunts hugged him and told him that they were proud of him, and then his uncle Bobby came up and hugged him. "G, you are something else, man."

Lakeesha stood by his side, and he held her hand and introduced her to everyone as his fiancé, and they all hugged and welcomed her into the family.

The next day the general came up from the Pentagon and gave G and Randall their Legion of Merits, signed by the President of the United States. G was a proud soldier that day.

The following day the family all attended their grandmother's funeral and said their goodbyes. They celebrated her life and hugged their grandfather when it was done.

The following weekend G and Lakeesha, were married in Baltimore at the family church, with Lakeesha's mom and dad in attendance . Everyone was very happy for both of them and wished them well for their future. When it was time for G to get out of the army, he received numerous awards and medals. The colonel told him he would always be welcome to come back if he ever wanted to, and he would recommend him to become an officer.

G and Lakeesha finished college with degrees from Morgan State and got good jobs downtown. G joined the American Legion Post 19 and became good friends with all its members. They were happily married and had two kids, a girl named Violet and a son named Gregory Jr. in whom he put all his hope that he would take his journey and not grow weary or take any detours.

A few years later on November 7, 2008, when G walked into the voting booth, he knew America with all its flaws was still the best hope for man. He knew that a city boy could grow up to be anything he put his mind to, and he knew the journey would continue for the home boy known as Baltimore Blue–Smile.